THE ORACLE

Randy,
Enjoy the Story.
Best

Michael H Sedge

PROLOGUE

CUMAE 427 BC

They had entered the tomb, and though she was more than two kilometers away, in her own underground shelter, she knew the seal of Olympus had been broken - for she had the power.

She had lived for centuries. The flesh of her face appeared twisted and gnarled. Her dark eyes, embedded behind tiny slit sockets, peered out like those of a vulture waiting for death. Her protruding lips parted slightly, allowing a putrid odor to escape her lungs. Hair no longer grew upon her ancient skull. No teeth filled her mouth. Her limbs, wrinkled and dwarf-like, had lost their use some seventy years earlier. She had not ventured from the dark, humid cave in decades. Time meant nothing, only existence was important.

The Cumaen people thought her a prophet. But she alone knew the true task the gods had burdened upon her. And now, the time had come.

"Let me die," she had often pleaded with the gods, to no avail. They needed her. Needed her alive. She alone knew the secret of the tomb. She alone held the key to its protection.

Now she felt it, heard it, sensed it. At last, her time had come. Sweat eased from her pores, trickling over the grotesque flesh - sending chilling tremors of excitement through her.

There were two of them, perhaps Greek. Her powers sensed an odor about them, though, that was unlike the Magna-Graecia peoples of Cumae. No, they were not of the Greek race. They were barbarians, and held no fear of this place. The tomb upon the hill was not sacred for them, though it held the body of Iosis, the only mortal love of Apollo.

After Iosis' death, even he, the god of music and beauty, could not rescue her from the arms of Hades. In his anguish, he had adorned the corpse with the riches of the gods, and placed the seal of Olympus over her resting place so that no human should ever gaze upon such wealth and beauty and be tempted to defy the gods.

But Apollo knew the fragility of men too well, so he endowed a young girl, who had fallen under his grace, with a psychic power over all men, to protect the tomb - she was the Sibyl.

The girl's family had come from Zakynthos, a tiny, wooded island not far from Ithaca. She had been only an infant when her father set sail along with Cira, her mother, and two brothers, Circeo and Ariele. They were one of many families who, because of political turmoil among the archipelago, left their homes and ventured to "New Greece", as it had come to be known.

They settled on a high mountain surrounded by the sea on two sides. The peninsula on which their new home was built extended to the south for six kilometers before it gave way to the limpid waters of the Mediterranean. To the north, the land extended into rich meadows, hills and forests. Eventually, should one venture long and far, the geological beauty became dramatic, snow-capped mountains where, some believed, the gods lived when they were away from their Olympian home.

On the opposite side of these giant covered slopes - so tales explained - was the land of the uncivilized, those who knew nothing of sea travel, true civilization, nor of the gods. They dressed in skins of animals they killed and devoured. They fought other tribes, and they quarreled amongst themselves. They were the barbarians, vicious beasts, without respect for tradition, learning, history, or even life itself.

The civilized, gentile girl had grown rapidly in the new land, the land which became known as Cumae. Though much of her time was spent playing with friends and wandering the meadows surrounding the village, she took care not to neglect the gods.

"Devotion to the gods," her mother often said, "comes before all else. The gods will protect you always, but you must never forget them."

And she never had.

Though she attended each temple regularly and with reverence, she secretly favored the temple of Apollo. It was as if he was with her constantly, in her thoughts, if not her presence. In the meadow north of Cumae she had secretly constructed her own temple to the god. Though merely made of crude stones and sand, the flowers that decorated it made it a work of beauty. It was here that Apollo spoke with her for the first time.

"Daughter of Hegos, child of Cira, you alone have shown a dedication worthy of my attention."

The voice came from deep inside an olive tree which stood just beyond her tiny, hand-built shrine. Upon hearing the voice, the girl began to tremble, for there was no one to be seen. Then, the gnarled and twisted tree, heavy with its burden of fruit, began to glow as if the sun itself had suddenly burst from its old, rough trunk. So radiant was the light, and so struck with awe was she, that the girl was forced to look away, despite a longing desire to continue her gaze.

From the heavenly glow emanating from the now-become-holy tree, a man-like figure emerged. "You alone have been chosen among all the youth. Only you are worthy of the gods."

The voice was soft, and at the same time bold, forceful, and it was also the voice of love. It was the voice that emerges from the lips of a loving father, a kindly mother. It contained authority, but was filled with certain comfort.

Her fear was gone, and as she looked upon this figure of perfection, love poured from her heart. She knew… *this* was Apollo.

And though he could read her thoughts, he did not reply. He merely smiled at the lovely child.

"You alone will be trusted with the knowledge. You alone will share the secrets."

Apollo extended his arm, placing his hand upon the girl's head of thick, crow-black hair that swirled in giant ringlets around her angelic face and strong, yet delicate, shoulders.

"Close your eyes that you might see," he said in a tone which seemed to spirit arrows of ecstasy into the girl's heart. She obeyed without question, and as she did, *images* - not one, not two, nor even a dozen, but hundreds, which rushed into thousands, then turned into millions, and became trillions - rushed through her mind's eye. She could see the stars, the planets, the galaxy, the universe and then the swirls of infinite universes extending into a never-ending void. Secrets of the sea, the land, and the gods themselves were suddenly known to her. She witnessed the future, and looked back at the past.

But above all, with the penetration of this knowledge, she realized the reason for her existence. She saw her fate.

Her mouth opened and...

Had it not been for the presence of the god, she might have screamed at the horror of what she had witnessed. Instead, a sudden rush of love passed from the heavenly being into her with such an intensity that she went limp, then swooned.

Hours later, her eyes again opened to the bright, glowing light. At first she thought that only seconds had passed, and that the god was still in her presence. Turning her head, the brilliant light subsided and she realized it was merely the sun.

The olive tree seemed to stand as it always had. The tiny, flower-covered shrine next to her appeared the same. Everything seemed unchanged. But it was not, and she knew it. She knew she would never be the same again, for a far destiny, one which included her, had been set into motion.

Many centuries had passed since her first, and only, encounter with Apollo. She realized, however, that he was with her always, guiding her, caring for her, giving her the power. Some of the images she had seen so many years ago had eventually come to pass. Not all of them, not yet, but most. And, now, she had become the horrible dwarfed creature of her vision.

She held guardianship over the sacred tomb of Iosis, held it until the day men would discover it, and die. This was the burden placed upon her by the gods. This was the price she paid for the powers they had invested her. It was her task to ensure that intruders to the tomb did not survive.

The powers had brought her fame. She was noted throughout all the lands touching the Mediterranean, even to tribes living on the continent to the south. Tales of her had spread throughout the known world.

Parents would consult her before choosing a spouse for their child. Farmers would come to her with questions of future harvests. Leaders of tribes and rulers of empires would bow at her feet as she recited the events of their future, warning them if they should avoid battle, encouraging them if destiny would award them a victory. Even the great Aeneas, hero of the Trojan War, had sought her out before entering the underworld.

Yes, she had enjoyed the power. But the passing years, decades, and centuries, had been a living hell.

Now, after 300 years of waiting, her senses had been aroused. The vision had appeared to her. The seal had been broken. They had found Iosis' resting place and the treasures of Olympus.

She whispered the mystical words without remorse. This was the moment for which she had waited so long. Once the invaders ceased to breathe human life, she would be free. Alas, free… she would be free to *die*!

"Oh Hades, mighty god of the underworld, hear me. Release the Furies of Evil upon the intruders of the tomb. Bring death to all men who walk the sacred hill which rises high above the sea of Poseidon; the hill that holds, beneath its clovered meadows, the treasures of the gods; the hill that disguises the tomb of the once-fair Iosis, who now stalks the shadowed paths of your realm. Hades, oh mighty Hades, brother of Zeus, hear me, the Sibyl, daughter of darkness. Come to my call."

Her tiny breasts, shrunken and shriveled over time, heaved spasmodically as words seeped from her lips. The chant echoed through the tunnel's hexagon-shaped corridor. The whistling winds carried the sound out of the cavern into the blinding light of day. Almost instantly, a harsh cold wind swept across the acropolis.

It was working. She could feel the presence about her. She could feel the existence of evil. The beams of wondrous, heavenly light that entered through the gouged-out oxygen shafts that alleviated the blackness and gloom of her domain suddenly vanished. Only the horrors of darkness prevailed. Still, she could see. Her eyes had long been accustomed to the dark. And, at this moment, she loved it. It was the darkness of triumph, the triumph of death.

Above her cavern, screams came from the Cumaens as the sky turned black. It was as if a giant demon had engulfed the blazing sun, taking the security of day and replacing it with the haunting, unknown darkness of night. A night unlike any other night in history. This night, terrors as yet unknown, suddenly swept over the fact of the earth.

She trembled with delight, laughing at her final duty. She was like a child, or even a young girl experiencing romance for the first time - though that was an emotion of which the gods had deprived her. Saliva ran from the corners of her warbling mouth as her leathery tongue moved to form words.

"Great evils of darkness, bring forth the revenge of the gods. Let no man that enters the tomb see the light of day. Go now, go. Destroy them! Destroy them! Let the blood boil within their veins. Melt their minds within their skulls. Burst their loins while they still live. Destroy them! *DESTROY THEM! GREAT EVILS OF DARKNESS, BRING FORTH THE VENGEANCE OF APOLLO!*"

The tomb was exactly two kilometers east of the Cumae acropolis. Its design was that of a vaulted spiral, rising slightly above ground level. On the northern side, half buried beneath the moist terrain was an arched doorway large enough to allow a single person entrance to the lower level. It was here, upon the heavy bronze door, that Apollo had placed the seal of Olympus. Unlike the simple locks used by the Greeks, the seal was a single mass of gold impressed into the door and its supporting frame, joining them together, much as if they were a single unit. The gold had been heated to a point so that it had not turned liquid, but was just soft enough to be locked into place without running or distorting. Then, with a force that only a god could possess, Apollo had brought the stamp bearing the seal of Olympus down upon the heated metal.

To a mortal eye - or mind - the design stamped into the gold seal would mean nothing. The symbols it contained, however, would have been as easily recognizable to a god as maps of the heavens, the routes used by the Olympians as they traveled the galaxies.

Behind the tomb's door were three steps leading to the center of the vault. From within, Magna-Graecia masonry skills were evident. Layers of tufa stone had been shaved into rectangular blocks and placed mathematically to form the perfectly round dome. The coffered ceiling was covered with stucco, concealing the rough stones. Frescoes depicting the four seasons decorated the inner walls, much as the paintings and frescoes of the Renaissance would adorn cupolas of the houses of worship more than a thousand years in the future. The highest point of the enclosure rose exactly two meters, then sloped gradually in towards the circular sides. Covering the floor was the mosaic which Apollo had brought from the palace of Zeus. The mosaic, consisting of gold, silver and jeweled tesserae, had been crafted by Metis, the muse of wisdom.

There was something magical in the work, its flowers, birds, and most of all, the enormous golden sun around which all other objects revolved. It was the mosaic of Undisturbed Time.

Now, however, time *had* been disturbed. The serenity - the very tranquility of time itself - had been broken.

The barbarians had begun climbing the hill, at first, to examine its military vantage. Knee-high meadow grasses swayed in the wind as they walked. They had admired the red poppies, with their coarse black-eyed centers, that grew wild over the distant slopes, casting a beautiful contrast against the green. They came upon markings indicating it was a holy place, but they only laughed and moved on. Then, quite by chance, they discovered the tomb. At the sight of the golden seal, greed overcame their original curiosity. Continuing to gaze, the lust for riches overwhelmed them. Who knew what riches lay beyond the already untold wealth offered by the seal alone? Sacking even a dozen of the richest villages would not have brought the value of such an object.

Despite their best determined efforts, the seal remained intact, denying entrance to the tomb and the greater riches that lay beyond.

"*THE HATCHET!*" cried the larger of the two men. "We shall have this gold and what lies beyond the door. No lock has ever resisted the blows of an Etruscan hatchet."

The warrior extended his burly arm, clad with brass wrist bands, and grasped the weapon's shaft with both hands. The weight of it alone would have brought a Cumaen to his knees, but the barbarian whirled the razor-sharp instrument as if it was a toy. It sliced through the air with a *whoosh*, coming down onto the seal with a resounding *WHUNK!*

The seal held.

WHUNK!

The force of the second blow separated the embedded gold emblem, and with the third and fourth attacks, the ancient seal gave way completely, falling, gleaming, to the ground.

As they shoved open the long-closed door, a shaft of hot, summer sun shot through the dank, musty dark, falling directly upon the chalky face of Iosis. As the vespers of fresh air tiptoed into the ancient chamber, the gentle waft of air pressed softly on the long-dead corpse, causing it to ever-so-slowly crumble into a fine talc-like powder which was lifted onto the breeze in a gentle swirl that danced lightly in the air about the sacred room.

Outside, the Etruscans gathered up the gold piece that only seconds before had held an Olympian seal. Then, slowly, they crouched to enter the shrine, one after the other. They had not seen the body disintegrate. Standing in the center of the floor was the bronze couch where Iosis had rested these many past centuries. The golden crown and precious gems that had adorned the body lay mingled with the remaining white dust. Beneath her metal resting place sat a chest over-flowing with gold and silver. It had been forged in the fiery workshop of Hephaestus, god of metalwork.

"It's ours!" bellowed Hexnigoff, the smaller and older of the intruders. He scurried about the underground room, grasping the crown and raking the gems into his hands with a sweep of his arms. "We're rich!" His creased and weathered face broke into a huge grin, and his eyes twinkled despite the dim light.

Stuffing as many of the precious objects into his pouch as it would hold, he reached for the chest, pulling it from beneath the bed. There was no lock, and as the lid fell back the old man's eyes bulged.

"Gold! Diamonds! Gems!" he shouted, then paused a moment, closed his eyes and shook his head, as if he would awake any minute from a dream and the riches would all be gone. But when he opened them it was all still there.

"WE'RE RICH!" he screamed. *"RICH!"* Digging his hands into the treasure, he leapt to his feet, precious stones skittering across the floor and coins dancing a dizzying circular jig about the room as he danced hysterically. Laughter burst from his lungs between bellows of, *"RICH, RICH, RICH!"*

From inside they could not see the changes taking place in the sky. In the excitement of their newly-discovered wealth, the initial subtle changes in air temperature were barely noticeable.

The younger Etruscan had remained silent throughout his companion's uncontrolled antics. After a while, though, Hexnigoff gained control over his emotions, and he sat on the floor idly sifting his hands through the treasure in the chest.

"Hexnigoff."

One last chuckle escaped Hexnigoff's lips as he turned to answer his partner. Then, the hysterical ecstasy was gone. Taking its place was a wide-eyed expression of terror. For he had turned just in time to see - but not avoid - the heavy hatchet that within an instant would not only pierce his skull, but would crush the bones as well.

But, we're rich... was the old man's last, questioning, thought before the sound of the bones in his head splintered the silence. Almost before the thought was completely finished, his brain was spilling out on either side of the glistening weapon. His death was instant. A crimson gush of blood vomited from his mouth. His eyes burst free from their sockets to dangle over each cheekbone. His legs flopped and the muscles of his shoulders pulsed violently.

Pulling the hatchet from the still-thrashing body, the barbarous assassin crossed the room to where the precious treasure rested.

His chest heaved up and down heavily, as it always did after a battle. Whether it was the murder of his companion, or the fact that the riches were his, and his alone, that caused the adrenaline to flow, he did not know. Nor did he care. All he wanted now was to gather up his new found wealth and be gone.

He pulled the pouch of jewels and coins from Hexnigoff's body and strung it over his shoulder. Then he turned his attention to the chest of riches.

Despite his strength, the weight of the jeweled chest would not allow him to carry everything. He decided he would just take what he could easily carry, and return for the rest.

Thunder clapped outside the underground vault and sunlight no longer shone through the tiny entrance. Yet the room was not dark. In fact, it seemed even more brightly illuminated than it had initially.

"The sun."

A look of horror crossed his heavily bearded face. He whispered the words to himself. Or so he thought. No sooner had the words been spoken than he felt a presence in the room - a presence he feared, and he feared little.

An eerie tremble eased along his spine as if some unseen person had run a finger down his back. He turned. No one. The forces of evil were invisible to his mortal eyes.

"No, no. It can't be. It can't *BE...*"

But it was.

There was light. And, yes, it did come from the sun. Not the heavenly sun, however; but the golden sun of the mosaic floor. It came from the sun of Metis. And as the rays become more and more brilliant, the temperature within the tomb suddenly flashed to an unbearable state.

The gold, silver and gems suddenly became too hot to hold, and they scattered across the floor as the barbarian's huge hands unclenched, jerking away from the burning treasures.

The door. I have to get to the door, he thought.

It was a good thought, a logical thought, but a thought that would never be carried out.

Despite his efforts to reach the opening at the far side of the room, it seemed to move further away. The temperature rose higher. Oxygen ceased to enter the room, and his lungs gasped for air, savoring every molecule they found. In one last effort, he thrust his hulk towards the doorway. In midair, however, he was suddenly whirled about, landing flat on the blazing tesserae sun. The flesh of his face began to sizzle, bubble and blacken upon the floor. His hands blistered and became coal-like. His beard vanished in a burst of white smoke, giving off a rotten smell. Hot singes began to corrode his clothing, not igniting for the lack of oxygen. Lying upon the artificial sun, he felt as if he were embedded in a white-hot anvil. He could not get away without removing half his face, but he could not remain there and live. He was in no position to make a decision to save himself, however. Other forces had control over the tomb, and his salvation. Though his thought was indeed rational, it was to be his last.

The oxygen level rapidly dropped below the level to support human life. A gasping sound emerged from his half-melted, charred lips. Through his blurring eyes the room began to spin, at first lazily, then faster, then faster, then faster still. A warm needle-sharp pain rushed into his consciousness and through his skull. He could feel himself expanding - the pain unbearable - until he felt, but did not hear, his head explode like an overheated melon. Gobs of flesh and tissue splattered stains onto the stucco walls and ceiling, adding distorted smears of color to the heavenly artwork. What remained of his body was slowly rendered to ashes over the white hot mosaic sun.

The forces of evil were no longer present. They had sought, and found, vengeance.

With the remains of the once-beloved Iosis gone, the riches of Olympus vanished, simply sped away to their original home. Now, only the tomb remained. The tomb of death.

High upon the Cumae Acropolis, light once again beamed into the Sibyl's cave. At the far end of the tunnel where a small room had been dug out, the Sibyl perched. Her eyes were closed. Respiration was no longer noticeable. Within her chest, though, the ancient heart continued to pump the sap of life through her veins. After a short while, this too ceased. Her body was at rest. But her soul could not die.

She had survived longer than any other human being. Time had been a great teacher. And the knowledge she gained, and the divine powers she possessed, had made her a goddess of the Cumaen peoples. To the human race, the mystical lady would live forever in verse and folklore. Of course, others would come to take her place, for the city needed a replacement to fill the tradition.

Yet, there could be only one true Sibyl: servant of the gods; watcher of time; the one who silently waited so long to perform her last task. It was for this that her spirit would continue to haunt the eerie cavern that, for so many years, had been her home. Now, however, her task completed, her unneeded body fell from its perch. Alas, the Sibyl had died.

Outside the weather had cleared; the clouds disappeared even more swiftly than they had come. The icy cold winds were replaced by a hot afternoon sun that warmed the earth. It was a beautiful day.

DAVID

(The Writer)
(1)
Naples, Italy 1986

Generally speaking, writing is one of the most peculiar occupations any person can hold. And, often, just as strange are the writers themselves. This is particularly so when pertaining to their work. At times it seems to possess them, hound them, haunt them. What was once a hobby now becomes a necessity. Their common lifestyle is traded for a typewriter - or computer - a ream of white, twenty-pound, bond paper, a thesaurus, a dictionary and a flashing cursor on a computer screen. Nothing else exists. It is their life. The nine-to-five working day is replaced by fourteen to seventeen hours of mental and emotional strain, anger and humor, laughter and tears, and at times, though seldom, satisfaction. Families are no longer the center of life. Food becomes secondary. The writer becomes trapped. Nothing matters but his work: words, phrases, articles, books. They mount into stacks. Half of the night is spent pecking out the sound of life, like a pianist creating a symphonic movement, which often becomes nothing more than a demonic litany. If time permits, what sleep there is often restless, and more often than not, filled with uneasy dreams that are often too, full of possible new ideas. Writers are gods, murderers, lovers, enemies, friends, and companions;

but only to the characters they have created in their fictional, and often, unreal worlds.

This was the world of David Jeffrey. For the past ten years writing had been his sole profession. Previously, he had served eight years as a public affairs officer for the US Navy, and leaving the military had been a difficult decision, for he genuinely liked his job, the travel, most of the people he worked with, and certainly the people he met. He particularly liked the fact that one of his jobs had thrust him into a position to meet many of the top names in the writing profession. This networking made his decision to leave the Navy easier, and had made his debut as a writer much easier. The gamble had paid off. And this new world of his was just that.

His world. He had created it, and he loved it.

Of course, there was also his other world: that with his wife, Jennifer, who, despite a hint of gray in her otherwise raven-black hair, was still a beautiful woman. Over the years he had learned to live with her drinking problem. He thought it had begun shortly after his discharge from military service. In reality, it had started several years earlier.

Jennifer had enjoyed the military lifestyle. It was, in fact, the only life she had known, having grown up the daughter of a naval officer. She had tried to convince him to "Stay Navy" as a recruiting poster advised, but he was determined to be a writer.

Having failed in her quest, the process of breaking away had left her bitter, and her drinking became more intense. Their marriage had suffered as a result and alcohol had compounded their other problems.

"A drink now and then," she had once told him, "helps me accept the fact that you've tossed away our friends and any hope for a 'real' future."

Though he disliked his wife in this state of mind, he told himself that it would pass with time, and became more and more ensconced in his own fictional worlds. He never really did take time to ensure that her excessive drinking had stopped.

It had not.

There was also another part of his real world, his tangible world. It was his daughter, Angelica, who was now becoming a lady, a poised, well-mannered young lady. He was proud of her. She was the daughter of perfection, never giving them any problems and obeying their every word. She was almost too good.

The only time David had really been dedicated to his family over the past ten years was when he broke away from his labors-of-love to spend time with Angelica. If there was anything that would bring him out of his creative world, it was her.

Jennifer, too, had noticed the attention her husband gave the girl. At first she was pleased. But as the girl grew older, the pleasure turned to jealousy, festering, eventually, to anger and a dislike so intense it bordered on hatred. In Jennifer's mind, Angelica had taken David, robbing her of the affection she wanted and needed. The increased emotional stress, combined with her excessive drinking, had not made for a happy home. David became reclusive, and Angelica began to spend more and more time with her friends, away from home. Jennifer, alone, had become the victim, or so everyone thought. The truth was, of course, Jennifer was a spoiled, self-centered, irrational drunk. In addition to her booze, she had found another way to give "meaning" to her life. That had started a while back too.

There were times when David sincerely wished he had more time to spend with his wife and daughter, but his work could not wait. Not even for a short while. He had to work. He wanted to work. He was a writer and he loved it. But it had also been the key which locked the door between him, his wife, and his daughter. They had never truly understood.

Among his contemporaries, David was a genius of the trade. His specialty was the craft of intermingled mysteries which had grown so popular over the past few years. The critics had been good to him, comparing his varied works to those of Elmore Leonard, Lawrence Block and P.D. James. He had won America's National Book Award for fiction and, in England, the Crime Writers' Association's Gold Dagger Award. He had won several mystery writers' awards too. For the most part, the critics and the public at large loved him.

"We give credit where credit is due," Carol Beemer, a Detroit Free Press reviewer, had told him. They had met during a writers' conference at Ball State University in Muncie, Indiana. David had been a guest speaker at the gathering, though he disliked crowds and rarely made personal appearances. But since he was living so far from the publishing world - amongst the antiquities of Italy - his agent, Jim Johnson, of Todd, Simpson, and Johnson Literary Agents, thought it might pick up sales if he took a working vacation in the United States.

"No big deal, Dave," Johnson had told him during a transatlantic phone conversation. "A couple of TV spots, a few radio call-in shows, and maybe an interview or two with the major print media."

So, when the opportunity arose, David took it, despite his personal reluctance. The trip did, however, increase sales.

This, in turn, accounted for the sale of motion picture rights to three of his books. And according to the latest report sent to him by Todd, Simpson, and Johnson, sales had nearly tripled since Paramount released the film version of *Velvet Dagger*, his last novel. David did not write the movie script, though the job was offered. Rehashing something he had already finished did not appeal to him. Besides, it would mean months in a Hollywood hotel, away from his family, and his beloved Italy. More important than that, it meant time away from his work. He did collect $469,000 from the motion picture clause of his contract, though. That, naturally, was after Todd, Simpson, and Johnson took their fifteen percent.

JENNIFER

(The Wife)

(1)

Jennifer Roberts was always being told how much she resembled her Italian mother. Her skin was smooth and dark. Even without washing it for a week, her black hair was satin-like. Her large, dark eyes glittered behind a set of tantalizing lashes. Physically, she had developed at a younger age than most girls. Shortly thereafter, she was flirting her firm, youthful breasts to attract the attention of the school-boys who, to that point had only fantasized of being with a "real woman" as Jennifer considered herself. Mrs. Roberts had openly discussed sex with her daughter. And, just as openly, her daughter had revealed that she knew as much - if not more - than her mother about the subject. It was at this point that Mrs. Roberts had a local physician give her a prescrip-tion - which she passed onto Jennifer - that would prevent any embarrassing slips.

"You have a reputation to think of," her mother had stressed. "And what about your father's career? What would people say if they thought the daughter of the NATO Public Affairs Officer was out with a different boy every night?"

The discussion usually reached a boiling point with this kind of talk. Jennifer normally ran out of the house, called her friends from the payphone in Arco Felice and ended up at a friend's apartment smoking pot and having sex. She often wondered afterwards, which pleasure was greater, that of the lovemaking or the fact that she was doing it to spite her mother.

She didn't give a rat's ass for her father's career. In fact, there was only one thing that she cared less about, that was what people thought - especially military people. Even living in Italy, she realized that the military was not the real world. People within "the system" lived differently from normal Americans, and she wanted no part of it. That is, until she met David Jeffrey, a handsome, mature, Navy lieutenant junior grade.

It was at the Allied Officers' Club on the Allied Forces Southern Europe, NATO, base in Naples. Jennifer's mother had insisted she come along.

"It will help the family image," she insisted, as if they had an image to be helped.

There was the usual buffet - steaks burnt on the outside, a sick red in the middle, and salad with brown-edged lettuce. Bobby Solo, the Italian Elvis, was the evening floor show, which, in Jennifer's opinion, was straight out of the '50s.

When David entered the club, Commander Roberts and his colleagues had already killed five bottles of Lambrusco and were working on the sixth.

"Dave. Dave Jeffrey." The young assistant public affairs officer squinted to see through the dim light.

"Come 'n' join us, boy." Roberts was feeling a buzz from the fermented juice of the grape and David knew it.

"Thank you."

"You know my wife."

"Yes, good evening."

"My son, Jerry, and this is my baby girl, Jennifer." David had already noticed her. Not, however, as the boss's baby girl.

"Pleasure," his steady hand extended to meet that of Mrs. Roberts and her son, but trembled as it eased towards the young woman. The table candles cast a glowing highlight over Jennifer. To David, she appeared to be in a haze, the princess of a dream he had many years before.

"You know all these other drunks, don't ya, Dave?" Commander Roberts said as a burst of laughter engulfed the table.

The lieutenant's eyes were still lost in the girl's beauty. The final remark had entered his brain but did not register.

"Sir?" Another roar burst from the intoxicated officers.

"Sit down, boy." Tears eased from the corners of the commander's eyes and his kidneys began to tingle with pain.

"Damn it, where is a chair for my assistant?"

"Here, Daddy." Jennifer quickly pulled a heavy, wooden chair from a neighboring table and slid it next to her own.

The commander smiled. "If the military acted that fast, we wouldn't have to worry so much about goddamn Middle East."

Once again the table was encompassed in an air of hysterics. All, that is, but David and Jennifer. Their minds were intermingled in the dreamlike atmosphere between them.

The evening seemed to race by, the hours simply evaporating. That brief encounter, however, was enough for them to realize they would see each other again.

It was 6:15 the following evening when the downstairs telephone rang in the Roberts' home. Lieutenant Jeffrey was the caller.

Jennifer had waited all day. She knew he would call, or at she least hoped so. Now she was at the receiver accepting his invitation to the San Carlo Opera - one place she would normally despise going.

"There's a performance of Verdi's *Aida*," came a soft, gentle voice in the girl's ear. But she did not care what was on the program. Her only thought was that they would be together.

The months that followed were like nothing Jennifer had ever experienced. Even her mother had noticed the difference. Jennifer attended the theater regularly with David; they took in art exhibitions, went on weekend tours offered by the base Travel Office, and occasionally, spent an evening at the "O" club, as David put it, politicking. Jennifer, in fact, for the first time, actually began to enjoy socializing in military circles.

David was unlike other men, who were only interested in her physically. Sex had always been her weapon, but with David it was not necessary. He was kind. Gentle. Sincere. And the idea of luring him into her web had never occurred to her.

They had known each other exactly five months the night David proposed. It was a hot July evening, a soft breeze easing across the Bay of Naples. They were riding along Via Posillipo when David quite unexpectedly stopped the Fiat 128, kissed her, and asked her to be his wife. At the time it had seemed the proper question. And, without thought, Jennifer gave what she considered the proper answer.

"Yes."

That evening, she gave him something else - herself. This was something she had never done before. Yes, sure, there had been lots of sex, but never any love. She discovered it was beautiful. She was his, not only physically, but spiritually, emotionally, and mentally. There was no doubt she loved him. And Jennifer knew David loved her so much that there would never be another woman in David's life.

The ceremony was a simple one. Just the immediate family - Jennifer's, that is. Everyone understood the Jeffreys not showing up. After all, Michigan was more than 8000 miles from Naples. Besides, the newlyweds would be spending two weeks of their four-week honeymoon, in the Great Lakes State.

When they did meet, Jennifer hit it off well with her new in-laws, especially David's younger brother, Jack. He had married two years earlier and his wife, Valerie, had lost a baby during the first year. Doctors had assured her, however, that she could have other pregnancies. On the return flight to Italy, Jennifer wondered how long it would be before she could write them of her own pregnancy.

The ob-gyn doctors at the Naval Regional Medical Center in Naples had said some women become pregnant immediately after going off the pill. Others remained affected for months, some years, after.

The first month of married life was like a dream come true. Jennifer kissed her new husband goodbye each morning, met him for lunch at the Allied Officers Club, and had dinner on the table when he arrived home. Then, only slightly more than a year after they were married, David was sent on temporary duty aboard the aircraft carrier, USS Theodore Roosevelt.

"It will only be for a week or two, honey," he had explained.

But, two weeks slowly dragged into three, then four, then into more than two months, and finally, Jennifer found herself alone for their second anniversary. David went from one Sixth Fleet ship to another, seeing Jennifer for, at most, one week between each transfer. The ships' movements were strictly classified, but her father fed her regular reports as to David's whereabouts.

At the onset of their marriage, and not fully knowing what her mother meant by "military widow," Jennifer had promised to be a faithful wife. Keeping her promise, she had found comfort in social activities - Allied Officer Wives' Clubs, Navy League, International Archaeological Society, and old friends, but with military transfers and all, Jennifer found all her old schoolmates moving back to the United States. So, it wasn't too long before she also found comfort in an occasional Bacardi and coke.

It was on such occasions, after consuming several of the later "companions," that her mind would turn to memories of pleasures she now longed for. She was alone, lonesome, and had a desire for human companionship so strong that it began to haunt her. She could visit her parents, but that was not the company she really wanted.

Determined to fight the fantasizing urges until David's next return home, she suddenly secluded herself from the outside world, not taking part in any of the activities that had kept her occupied before. Now she was drinking until she no longer remembered what she did or who she was.

It was a lonesome Friday night and Jennifer had already killed her fifth Bacardi and coke as the sun settled slowly into the Mediterranean, looking like a huge orange ball that became a half ball, then just a small partially round object that sank into the cool blue waters before disappearing. Out the window of their home and off in the distance, the shadows of the islands of Capri and Ischia could be seen. The weather was so soft it almost seemed as if it held texture in the air. Jennifer was nodding a bit as she gazed out into the Bay. It was a wonderfully peaceful evening and the sunset had been so beautiful that part of the melancholy that had settled around her was dispelled. She reclined on the blue-green chaise longue and had just dozed off when the harsh jangle of the phone, with its shrill ring, jolted her awake.

"Pronto," she responded, almost in a whisper of perfect Italian.

"Jenny? Hi, it's Jerry."

"Jerry?"

"Yeah, Jerry Knutson. Remember me? What's new?"

She was stunned, momentarily speechless. Jerry and she had attended many parties, both arriving alone, but always leaving together. That had been long before David. Before her marriage.

Before...

"Hey, still there, Jenny?"

She knew there was only one reason he would be calling. In a small American community like that in Naples word travels fast.

He knows David's out of town, she thought.

The thought, while causing a tinge of guilt, excited her.

"Yeah, I'm here...and not doing much, to answer your question. You're the last person I expected to hear from. Is there a particular reason for this unexpected call?" She began to play the flirting game she had been so good at only a few years before.

"I hear your old man is out of town."

"And?" She loved the thoughts that were racing through her mind.

"We're having a party at Giulia's in Lago Patria and wondered if you'd like to drop in."

"I don't think so, Jer," she lied and, immediately wondered why she had said that. Of course she wanted to go. But David... what if he found out?

"Hey, come on," his voice was teasing now. She hated to be teased almost as much as she loved to tease others.

"The guys said you wouldn't come. They said a woman's never as good after she's married."

She was both excited and angry. The table had turned and it was Jerry who now held the upper hand. But she would not give in. Her emotions were torn between lust and love. She owed David her loyalty... but almost desperately desired affection.

"Jerry, I can't!" Jennifer slammed the phone onto the hook. She was trembling and instinctively reached for the Bacardi bottle. She glanced at the eight-by-ten wedding picture of her and David on the polished desk. Perspiration trickled from her underarms. She had made the right decision. She had done the right thing.

Two hours of quiet solitude had passed since Jerry's call, and she had dozed off once again. Then, again, the shrill voice of the ringing telephone broke the silence.

It's Jerry, she thought, and began trembling with excitement as she lifted the receiver.

"Hello." There was a long silence. It was not Jerry, as she had suspected... or hoped?

"Hello?"

"Hi, hon."

"David?"

"Yeah, baby, how are you?" The sound of his voice was like life after death. There was so much to ask that she didn't know where to start. Most of all, his voice brought her emotions under control.

"Jenny. Jenny, can you hear me?"

"Yes. Yes. I can hear you. I'm fine. I'm just fine now. Where are you?"

"Barcelona."

With the loud music in the background, she barely made out his last word.

"Where?"

"Bar-ce-lo-na. We're leaving tomorrow, but I can't tell you where we're going. You know, hush, hush."

"When will you be home, David?"

He began to laugh and Jenny could feel her emotions rising. This time not for love, or passion, but in anger.

"David!"

"Sorry, honey. One of the guys here is drunk and really making an ass of himself."

There was a silence, all except the music through the receiver.

"Still there, Jenny?"

"I said, when will you be home?"

"Hell, Jen, I really don't know. We've got this exercise coming up. Maybe next month."

She was on the verge of dropping the receiver. She wanted him there now. She needed him now, not next month. Tears filled her eyes and the ice in the glass made tinkling sounds as her hand trembled.

"Jenny, I have to go, baby. I'll see you as soon as I can, okay?"

"But David, I..."

"I know, honey, I miss you too. If you get lonely, why not stay with your mom for a few days? I love you, Jenny."

"I love you too, David, but..."

"Okay, baby. Ciao!"

"David I..."

The line was dead.

"...love you. I love *you*." Her voice trailed off until it became a whimper so soft that it faded to nothing as she sat alone in the dark stairwell.

By ten o'clock the once full Bacardi bottle was more than half-gone, and Jennifer had been lost in drunken-thought for more than an hour. She walked across the room and picked up the telephone receiver. Drunken rage had taken over her senses. She could destroy everything in the house, but that would be too easy.

"Go to your mother's," she mimicked his words in a whisper. "Fuck you, David! I'll show him where I go and where I don't."

The phone dropped out of her fingers, causing a squeaky laugh to emerge from her lips.

"You're drunk, sweetheart." She laughed again as her mind answered, "They'll like you just the same."

Her fingers found the telephone dial first, her eyes focused on it second. Six-five-two-six-one...

"Hello."

"Giulia!" Jennifer yelled into the receiver. "Hi, this is Jenny." There was a pause as she listened.

"Me? I'm fine, just lonely. A little bird told me that you're having a party tonight," her voice slurred.

(2)

Much had taken place since that night in their early marriage. David had left the military, become a prestigious writer, and their daughter, Angelica, had been born. Her husband never found out about the events that took place while he was in Barcelona, or any of the other affairs she had since. In fact, David could no longer satisfy her. She acted out artificial orgasms on those rare occasions when they had intercourse, but there was no real emotion. She had gotten into the habit of searching for men to satisfy her drunken lust at least once a week, if not more often. This evening was no exception.

The light was dim, but even so, she could tell he was good-looking. He didn't look Italian. Perhaps he was a tourist. He offered her a drink, which she accepted. After a few minutes of small talk, she felt the desire growing between her legs. She had to have him.

ANGELICA

(The Daughter)

(1)

Angelica Jeffrey had been going steady with Randy Fitzgibbons for three months. He was a senior, tall, with wavy blond hair, and piercing blue eyes. He was also the captain of the Naples American High School track team. They'd gone through the usual courtship rituals - hand-holding, close-mouth kissing, moving to a slip with the tongue and finally into the petting stage. Angelica was shy about sex, though her well-developed figure often drew the glances of much older men. She felt that any kind of affection between a boy and girl should be done in private, with tenderness and love. Because of this she had achieved a reputation around school as a "good girl".

Randy had always respected her wish to not make their personal desires a public display, other than holding hands and an occasional peck on the cheek.

They had their regular "make-out" spots, as the other kids called them. There was the road leading to the NATO beach, which Angelica preferred until the warmer weather brought out the swimmers. Then they moved to the quiet solitude of the Astroni game preserve, just a short distance from the Naval Support Activity in Agnano, west of Naples. This was the perfect location, full of trees, and no adults to interrupt anything that they might consider immoral for a girl still in high school - even if it wasn't wrong to teach it as a required subject.

There was only one problem with the reserve - the problem they faced this particular Saturday. It closed at dusk. That meant they would be trapped inside if they got carried away and didn't watch the time.

"Do you want to go or not?" Angelica could tell Randy was getting disgusted with her indecision.

"They'll be closed by the time we get there."

"Well, what *do* you want to do?"

"I don't know. Let's just drive around."

Randy had thought of that, but the Impala ate so much gas. His dad let him use the car with the stipulation that he buy the gas, which was $4.89 a gallon with the current lira exchange rate. It pissed him off that all the military gas coupons were hoarded by his dad. If he could get some of those he'd only have to pay a buck-fifty a gallon, only slightly more than people were paying stateside.

"Well?" Angelica persisted. "Are we going for a drive or not? There's a good movie at the base at 6:15 if you want to go."

"Jeez, Angie, first you say you want to get away from people, then you want to go for a drive. Now you want to see a friggin' movie. What *do* you want to do? What*ever* you *want* to do, we'll *do!*"

"I said let's go for a drive, and you just sat there like a jerk."

It was going to be one of those nights, and they both knew it.

Randy knew they could go for a drive after the movie, but the three dollars he had in the front pocket of his worn Levis wasn't enough to pay for gas and take in the film too. And he really wanted to be alone with her. He had made good progress in the past month, though it had been a long, patient task. Angie wouldn't even kiss him until the fifth date. This girl's an antique, he had thought. But eventually, she came around. Then it took another month to cop a feel of her boobs. They weren't anything great, still developing and all, but he liked the feel of the hard nipples. In the last two weeks he had taken the big step - getting his hand into her pants. Sure, she resisted at first, but she liked it. At least she seemed too.

Tonight was the night. He was determined. It had been nearly three months, plenty of time, even for a nice girl like Angie. If a guy couldn't get past the feeling stage in three months, he'd better find a new ball game. That's what the guys thought anyway. They called him a fool, but he'd have some things to tell on Monday.

"Get in," he said, flipping a thumb towards the blue Impala. "We'll drive around."

Angelica climbed in and slid next to Randy as best she could, considering the bucket seats. She could tell he was angry. She liked the large American car but hated the seats, which made getting close so uncomfortable. Cuddling close to Randy as he maneuvered the massive machine between Fiat matchboxes made her feel more feminine. Perhaps dependent was a better word. In either case, she liked the feeling.

Neither of them spoke as the car raced up the Via Domitziana towards Pozzuoli. By the time they had traveled seven miles and passed Parco Cuma, a seed of thought had blossomed in Randy's mind.

"You ever been to Cuma?"

"What?" Angelica had closed her eyes and gone into a day-dream-like state under the comfort of her boyfriend's arm.

"Have you ever been to Cuma?"

"We went there a few years ago for a school outing. Kind of dull. I mean, after you've seen so many ruins they all start to look alike."

"Never been there at night, huh?"

"You're crazy. Who'd want to go there in the dark? First, the place is closed. Second, it must be plenty scary."

The Impala's engine settled into a smooth rumble as Randy turned off the main highway onto the narrow Via Vecchia Cuma, which led to the ruins of the ancient acropolis.

"You don't have to go in through the gate," Randy said. "There are hundreds of other places to get in. Mike Freeman said that he goes there all the time with Debbie."

"Really? What if they got caught?"

"Who's going to catch them? The only one there's this old guy who leaves about six."

Once again the automatic transmission downshifted as Randy reduced their speed. The headlight beams flickered through the trees as Randy turned right and onto the 200 yard entrance to the ancient settlement.

"Randy, where are we going?"

"Just for a drive," he smiled, shrugging off her question, knowing exactly where they were going.

"You know, Cuma was the first Greek city in Italy. In those days it was called 'Cumae,' with an 'e', not like they spell it today."

"You're just a regular encyclopedia, aren't you?" Angie giggled.

"No, I did a report on the place for Sampson's history class," he joined her laughter, making both of them feel a little better.

"They even wrote about Cuma in that book...what the hell's the name?"

"Randy."

"Oh, sorry. What the *heck's* the name?"

The tires softly squealed, much like a scared pig, but muffled, as Randy turned right into the parking lot. Large oak trees surrounded the asphalt-paved area, giving them a feeling of seclusion so complete it felt almost as if it were, instead, isolation.

"Anyway," he continued, turning the ignition key to the off position. "This is really a famous place."

"Who cares?" asked Angelica, pulling his head down so that their lips met.

A surge of excitement raced through Randy. But he couldn't do it here. Anyone could make out with a girl in a parked car. He had to have something special to tell the guys. And that something was already planned.

"It's still early," he said, breaking their embrace. "Let's go for a walk."

"A walk? Where to?"

"Around the ruins."

"You're crazy."

"C'mon, you scared?"

"No, but..."

"Then let's go."

Randy yanked the keys from the ignition, slid out the door, tugging at Angie to follow, but then said, "Angie, there's a flashlight in the glove box3. Grab it, will you?"

Flashlight. Ruins. Walk. She thought Randy had been out of his mind when he, and a couple of his friends, went swimming in the fountain at Piazza Municipio in downtown Naples. But now! This was the icing on the cake.

Just the same, she found herself reaching for the chrome-handled flashlight. Once outside, she handed it to Randy.

"We can't use it until we get inside," he said. "If we do, someone might see us."

"Come on Randy, I don't want to go in there."

"There's nothing to be afraid of. I'll be with you. Besides, it's nice inside. Like a park."

"I've never been to a park without lights before."

"Look how bright the moon is, Angie. You could almost read a newspaper out here." He turned his hand slowly back and forth allowing the moonlight to embrace his hand. She could even see his class ring on his finger.

"An-gie." His voice was soft, sweet, and it did exactly what he had hoped.

"Okay, but stay next to me, and don't let go of my hand."

Getting in was a simply a matter of stepping over a chain, which was meant to keep out cars, not people. Inside, they made their way along a brush covered trail until they came to a clearing surrounded by pines. It was awash in the moonlight and she could see detail in the rocks and even the trees.

Randy had been right, Angelica thought. The full moon through the trees made a romantic setting. Together they stopped to look upon the picturesque patterns and, in the distance, the moonlight sparkled and twinkled on the waves across the open Mediterranean. It was easy to imagine how the early Greek settlers must have enjoyed this same sensation. Then...

"Come on, Angie."

...Randy broke the peaceful atmosphere.

"Where are we going? This is a nice place."

"Not much further, we're almost there."

Soft shadows eased across the now wide path as they headed towards the southern edge of the ruin site, a cat sat contentedly licking its paws in one of the shadows. And though the flickering shapes sometimes frightened Angelica, she was glad there was no need to use the single-beam flashlight. She had begun to relax, and was actually enjoying the trip into the park. This moonlight stroll was really becoming pretty good. She had fallen into step with Randy, their arms circled around one another.

Then Randy came to a halt, just in front of a huge dark hole cut into the stone face of a rock hill. It was a tunnel.

"Ever been in here before?" His voice was nearly trembling with excitement, but Angie did not seem to notice.

"Yes...but I don't want to go in there... not *now!*" She knew well of the cave of the Sibyl. It was one of the highlights of the Cumae site, and tourists traveled from the world over just to see the odd-shaped cavern which, according to legend, had once been the home of an ancient woman who lived for centuries guarding the mythical tomb of Hades, or something like that. The exact details slipped from the girl's memory at that moment.

Randy pulled the flashlight from where it had been tucked into his trousers and flipped it into the ready position. A shaft of bright, radiant light pierced the blackness, cutting the darkness and reflecting off the smooth-cut cavern walls.

"C'mon," Randy whispered happily as he pulled on Angelica's hand. "You're not afraid, are you?"

"No. Well… maybe a little. I just don't think it's a good idea to go in there. Especially with the place closed. What if someone catches us?"

"What if they do? The most they could do would be to ask us to leave. Come on, there isn't anyone around anyway."

Aiming the light into the tunnel, Randy moved into the depths of the slightly misty cave. Strangely, he briefly thought, the breeze seemed stronger here in the tunnel. As the teenagers moved closer to the once-sacred room at the cavern's end, the wind whispered in murmur, almost like a voice of warning through the darkness.

"*RANDY?*" hissed Angelica. "I don't like it here. Randy… Randy…*Randeeeee…*" she hissed softly. "Let's go!" she stated more firmly. Her not-so-loud, though near trembling cry bounced about the ancient cavern like some form of reverberating percussion in the damp, hollowed-out rock.

"*Shh,*" was the boy's only response.

"Shine the light down here! Here! By my foot!"

The flashlight beam enveloped the girl's suede Hushpuppies.

"What?"

"I thought something ran over my foot."

Randy scanned the area they had just walked past with the light. A tiny tree branch lay in the direct path that Angie had taken.

"You felt that branch. It brushed your foot. That's all."

"Let's go back, Randy." Her tone had been almost pleading. Now, she was begging.

But his mind was made up. A little further and they would be there.

"We're almost at the end. Look," he pointed the light in the direction they were heading. "You can see the end."

She didn't know why she had agreed with him, maybe she was just as crazy as he was. Or maybe it was because she loved him. Of this, she was sure. And when you love someone, you had to make sacrifices. That's what her father had once told her...but that had been about her mother's drinking problem. In any case, she now, suddenly, found herself agreeing to Randy's crazy obsession with reaching the end of the cave.

"Okay, but stay close to me." She reached out, sliding her arm around his back. "Put your arm around me."

"You're scared."

"Shut up, if you want me to make it to the end…. go on, go ahead, let's get it over with."

If Angelica had seen Randy's grin at that moment, she may have changed her mind. But it was swallowed by the darkness. For him the hard part was over. They were almost there, and he was sure she would not run out on him now.

At the end of the long, narrow tunnel a large room had been hollowed out. It was here that the legendary Sibyl supposedly spoke with the gods during the time of the Greeks. Around the edge of the semi-circular grotto was a ledge extending out about ten inches.

"See," Randy's voice was livelier now that they had reached their destination. "They even carved out a place for us to sit."

Angelica, still clinging tightly to him, sat on the ledge next to him. The wind could not be heard so distinctly now, not as it had when they first began their gradual descent into the cave. It was, in fact, quiet. Silent. Randy had his arm around Angelica, and in the stillness she felt protected. But when he pulled her a bit closer and she could feel the warmth of him through his shirt, the reason why Randy had wanted to come to this eerie place now agitated her thoughts. And the answer was beginning to dawn on her.

"Randy, why did..."

"*Shh*," he whispered softly, interrupting her. He turned her face towards him and kissed her gently. It began as a soft, warm kiss that became a long kiss, which turned into a hot tongue-teasing test of passion.

Was this why he had brought her here? Angelica trusted him. After all, they had been together three months and Randy had plenty of opportunities to make love to her. But here - here she could scream and nobody would ever hear. No. Not Randy. She could control him. She had always done it before. He was just enjoying her as far as he could. Like he had many times before.

Content with her reasoning, Angelica relaxed and let herself fall to her own desires. Neither of them had noticed that there was suddenly a slight increase in the wind in the tunnel.

"Mmmmm. Randy, *uh-uh*." He had reached the furthest point he had ever gotten with her. The zip of her jeans was open, his exploring fingers gently roamed inside her delicate lace-trimmed panties. He lightly caressed her pouting lips with his fingers. Angie had thrown off her usual taboo and had ventured inside Randy's pants with her own hand. Her new discovery excited her. She had not thought he would be so hard. Though she continued to whisper words of resistance - words interspersed with soft moans of delight - she knew this would be the place where she gave into him. They had waited long enough.

"*Ohhh*, Randy. Oh, yes… *yessss!*"

Suddenly, as the last desire to resist left her, Angelica felt a harsh chill flow into her. She had had her eyes closed ever since Randy first kissed her, and as her own passion grew it reduced her awareness of the once frightening surroundings. She had dedicated all her concentration on him and the delicious feelings he was creating in her. Now, though, her eyes suddenly snapped open. There was something strange about this place that she could not see. The feeling of being watched - laughed at, ridiculed - was surrounding her, suffocating her. She knew it was ridiculous, but still the feeling was there.

"Randy, *stop!*" she hissed sharply. "I want to go. I want to go *now*. There's something here."

"Come on, Angie. That's silly. There's nothing here. It's okay. It's okay. Besides, you know I love you."

"I know you do, but I don't want to stay here. Don't you feel it? Let's go someplace else. You can do whatever you want there. I want it too, but... *please*, let's leave this place!"

Angelica noticed that now, the wind that had begun swirling around the tiny cavern. She could feel something in the room. A presence. Something real. Something inhuman. She could sense it hovering over them. Watching. Listening. Waiting. She began to tremble.

Randy felt only Angelica's moist womanhood; sensed only his desire for her. In his passion, he had dropped the light, and now its ray bounced off the rock wall in a tiny circle and died. Though he did not feel the change in the atmosphere of the grotto, he did feel a change in Angie. It was strange. One minute she had been great, willing, pliable and obviously enjoying herself. Then, she changed. Became rigid, scared almost. What the hell was wrong with her?

The sensation became stronger and now Angelica began hearing voices. They came softly at first, almost as if from a dream, soft, haunting, floating, unreal, ethereal. And yet, at the same time, the words were clear, but carried no meaning for the girl.

"The soul cannot die. It will survive forever. The soul cannot die. It will survive forever. The soul cannot die. It will survive forever..."

The words echoed in a continuous rhythm. A rhythm cold, mystical, mantra like. There was more chanting inside her head, a hypnotic chanting that she neither liked nor disliked. The words floated on the wind, swirled about her brain, engulfed her entire being.

Randy knew it was no use trying further. She was completely detached from him now. They had been together long enough for him to realize that. Besides, he had gotten even further than he had expected, and had also discovered, to his surprise, that Angie wanted him too. She too had a desire - for him.

Maybe it was the place that stopped her? *He* didn't feel any difference in the cave. Sure, it was a little scary, but Angie was acting as if a ghost or something had slithered from a wall, or jumped from the floor. He'd gotten what he wanted. He had actually made out with her. Petted in fact, inside the cave... the guys would die on Monday when he told them that they had made out in the cave of the Sibyl.

He got up, crammed himself back into the proper place and closed his open fly. Angelica was still on the ledge, trembling, staring into the darkness where the voice - unheard by Randy - continued its harmony.

"Okay, let's go," he said, picking up the flashlight.

The words instantly brought Angelica back to reality. Jumping to her feet, she adjusted her pants and took a step forward.

"Hurry, Randy, I'm scared." She was no longer embarrassed to admit her fear as she had been earlier. Even the presence of the stronger, slightly older boy could not calm her now.

The tunnel seemed longer than it had on the way in and the voices followed Angelica through the shaft. She felt a need to hurry even more, and she was almost desperate to pee. Escape was perhaps a better word than hurry from this place. Yes, she had to *escape* from this place. Like Lot's wife, though, she too wanted to look behind, but the thought that she might see someone, or *something*, waving goodbye, kept her from doing so. In fact, it made her walk even faster. Randy clutched her hand, and by the time they had reached the mouth of the cave, Angelica was nearly running, pulling him along behind her. Once outside, the voices ceased, but the girl kept up her pace until they had reached and entered the car, and locked the doors behind them.

Randy had taken her directly home. The short ride had been one of silence. Memories of the voices continued to churn in Angelica's mind while Randy thought only of how close they had been to having sex. The thought gave him a sudden rush of excitement.

Now, lying in the safety of her bed, she couldn't remember if Randy had kissed her good night or, for that matter, if she even cared. She could only recall the eerie sensations she felt in the cave of the Sibyl and the echoing words...

"The soul cannot die. It will survive forever."

She knew it would be some time before she could sleep. She also knew that nightmares would plague her for a long time to come.

DAVID

(1)

Yes, David Jeffrey had loved writing, once. But in the last year he had begun to slow down. Where the words once flowed onto the pages, he now sat for hours contemplating every sentence. Secretly, he wanted to give up this life. He had not yet informed his family, but his mind was made up.

Like many writers, David Jeffrey kept his personal writings apart from those for publication. His were in a large blue-covered *Writer's Diary* within the top drawer of his oak desk. It had become a habit for him to make a daily entry just before going to bed, and today was no exception. The house was quiet now and he allowed his thoughts to roam. He began to write:

Jennifer and Angelica are asleep. They've been in bed for hours. It's 1:02 a.m., but I don't feel tired. In fact, I feel rather good. Relieved, I guess, is a better word. The last book is now completed. No more rewriting. No more picking at my brain like a scavenger for unknown words in the garbage heap. It's done.

I can now spend the time I want with my family. Time that has long been neglected.

Jennifer has been acting peculiar lately. Perhaps I am wrong? I mean, how does one judge another's peculiarities if they only see that person one or two hours a day? She's been going out more than usual, I think. And her drinking is heavier. The smell of alcohol fills the bedroom at night, when she is in a deep sleep. I wonder what she dreams...

All of this will change now. I'll see her and Angelica all day. We have enough money to last the rest of our lives, and Angelica's. We can go on picnics. Take in a few operas. Cruise the Med. Angelica has always wanted to see Palma, now she can have her wish. Maybe a trip to London next month would be good for Jennifer? She'll be so surprised to hear about my retirement. I wanted to give up writing long ago, but my agent had persuaded one more novel out of me. So the retirement plans were put aside. But now I can be the husband and father I should've been for so many years. It isn't too late, you know. I mean, I'm still young.

Diary, it's been a pleasure. But it's an even greater delight to bid you farewell.

David Jeffrey.

David never wrote in his blue-covered *Writer's Diary* again. Nor did he ever officially retire.

SURPRISES

(1)

In their intoxicated state, they caused a great racket coming through the heavy wooden door. First, she could not get the key into the lock, and there was a great deal of scraping, clinking, and jingling which turned into rattling, bumping, and thumping which was all interspersed with frequent cursing in two languages. Deeply entrenched in his final diary entry, however, David sat in the library at the opposite end of the villa completely unaware of their presence.

"Shh, you wanna wake up the dead? *Ah, bello.*" Even drunk, she played the luring role of a whore.

It wasn't the first time. She had had a number of men in the house while her husband was preoccupied behind closed doors, making mental love to the characters in his book. It had become a game to her. The chance that she might get caught made it all that much more exciting.

A shuffling sound came from behind the white door which led to Angelica's bedroom.

"What's that?"

"Ah, don't worry. It's my daughter," Jennifer giggled. "It won't be long before she's bringin' home studs like her mamma."

"And your husband?" Even in his drunken state the man she had picked up at Angelo's bar had a sense of awareness about him.

"Don't worry 'bout him either. He's working." He'll work all night on that damned book of his, she thought. "It's just you and me sweetheart." Her hand slid along his chest, slowly easing downwards. "Think about me, baby. I want all of you on me. All of you in me. I want your body and your mind."

"Okay, baby. Whatever you say."

He drew a half-filled bottle of Johnny Walker Red to his mouth and gulped freely, a little dribble running down his chin. Then, his lips were on hers. Their tongues clashed, darted, thrust, mingled.

Kissing, they slowly, drunkenly moved up the stairs towards the master bedroom - clinging, alternating hands, to the rail as they went.

Closing the diary, a huge surge of self-satisfaction encompassed David Jeffrey. Washed all over him. He had experienced the same sensation with the completion of each book. Not as strong, however. This time he felt...he felt serene. His fingers ached at their very tips. The center of his spine felt kinked from the long stretch - thirteen hours - at the typewriter. Numbness filled his right leg, causing an aching throb deep inside the leg. Dark circles had begun to appear long ago - unnoticed - under his strained eyes. Yet, he was happy. Perhaps happier than he had been in years. Perhaps happier than he had ever been. He had produced more than 15,000 words during a three-day marathon of writing. And he had produced some of the finest writing he had ever put on paper. For the first time in a year, the words seemed to flow, slowly at first, then more rapidly. Finally, his hands were unable to keep pace with his creative mind. But now, his last work completed, he had made his final diary entry and felt like celebrating. Taking the pack of MS cigarettes from the top of the desk, he tapped lightly on the bottom and retrieved one of the three stalks that protruded from the opened top. He rarely smoked. Italian cigarettes lacked the taste of the American brands. But, then again, this was a festive occasion. A cup of tea, perhaps? Yes, why not?

Before leaving the library he placed the paperwork into neat stacks upon the desk, replaced the books - including his diary - into the tall mahogany wall unit and punched the off switch on the NEC monitor with an extended index finger. He left the IBM computer running twenty-four hours a day. He then turned off the lights and quietly closed the door, not wanting to wake his wife or daughter.

The library entrance went into the corridor leading directly into a large antique filled living room. A double width semi-spiral staircase rose upwards on the far left. To the right, a large pine door, painted white, marked the villa's main entrance. On the opposite side of the room was Angelica's bedroom. The door was ajar. David glanced inside. Everything seemed to be locked in a peaceful sleep.

The kitchen was next to the girl's room on the right. David sighed as the fluorescent light flicked twice, then illuminated the completely tiled room.

"That's better," he whispered to himself. "The tea? The tea? Where the hell did she move the tea?"

Just as he found the blue and red tea box, the night silence was broken by the sound of shattering glass. The noise had come from upstairs. David stopped. Listened. Nothing. He walked out of the kitchen to cross the cool marble of the living room floor, and stopped, listening. Nothing. He began climbing the stairs, clutching in the darkness for the banister's support.

Then, he stopped.

A distant slit of light shown from under the master bedroom door. But that was not why David now stood, frozen, on the last step of the stairs. In addition to the light, laughter was coming from the room. Jennifer's laughter. And loud whispers. She was not alone.

Slowly, in an almost dreamlike state, David scaled the remaining step and stood on the large parquet landing.

"Forget the damn mirror, I'll clean up the mess later. I need you to finish me now!"

"Shh, oh... oh, baby." This time the sound was deep. Masculine.

"Mmmmm, mmm." The murmurs once again took the sound of his wife's voice.

The sounds alone gave away what he would find on the other side of the door. For some time, however, he remained standing, listening. A surreal, almost dreamy, trance-like feeling engulfed him. His emotions rocked. Indecision tore at him.

What should he do? Open the door to discover Jennifer and her lover? Stay where he was and listen? Go back downstairs? Leave completely? His mind became boggled by the choices. It was as if a scene had emerged from one of his novels to become true - only this time, he was one of the characters.

"*Oh, oh, ohhhhh!* Go, *bello*, GO!" Jennifer's voice ripped the stillness. The thought of her in bed with another man suddenly sent a surge of jealous rage through David's mind. At the same time, though, it excited him sexually. Maybe it was that which kept him riveted where he was.

"Okay. Do *me*. Do *me*. Do *me*. *Do me* now! Yes... yes! Like that... like that... like that! Rub it. Rub it! A*hhhhh*....yesssss...

ahhhh...rub it. Rub it! Rub it... rub it goddamn it! Rub it! That's it... that's it. Faster... faster... a little faster... faster... yes... yes... That's it... that's it... *ohhhh*, that's it, that's it... don't stop... don't stop... don't stop... don't stop... yes... yes... yesssss! *Ahhhhhh!!!*"

David could wait no longer, he needed no further prompting, for while Jennifer's gasps of pleasure and her words of lust had brought the desire bursting within his loins, the sounds of her unknown partner had had an opposite effect.

David felt his face become taut, forming into a red mask as he thrust his extended his arm toward the door latch. *Amazing*, he thought, *it's not locked.*

Smoothly, silently he swung the door open. In their mutual lust they did not see - nor, at that point, would they have cared about - the intruder, for at the exact moment that David swung the door open man and woman simultaneously reached their peaks.

Jennifer was literally screaming now. "Go! You son-of-a-bitch go...! Switch! Switch! Switch! Switch now! Switch to your tongue! Switch to your goddamned tongue! There was a moment's pause as Jennifer's lover slid round quickly to thrust his face between her wide-spread legs. Her back arched and her pelvis raced, matching his the movement of his darting, stabbing tongue.....

"*Urhhhhhhhhh!*"

The musty smell of sex and the raw smell of liquor rushed around David, overwhelming him. Even though he had known what to expect, he was shocked by the sight. Upon the king-sized bed the husky man - whom he could not fully make out - suddenly rolled from his position with his face thrust between the woman's parted legs to lie naked on his back. His erect penis thrust into the air.

David's wife rolled over to take the man's erect penis in her mouth - their bodies rolled in opposite directions and now they were reversed, him beneath licking her again, her above, sucking his erect member.

David could not move. He could only stare. They *still* had not noticed him. And the sounds of their lovemaking, along with the spectacle, were creating waves of excitement in him.

Jennifer was moving uncontrollably now.

"*Mmmmm. Oh, oh, ohhhhhhh!*" She rocked her pelvis back and forth as spasm after orgasmic spasm rocked her. Her head bobbed back and forth establishing the same rhythm as she was forming with her heaving belly and thighs. It was obvious the man had erupted into her mouth for she was making deep gulping noises that matched the pace of her thrusting hips and bobbing mouth.

As the last spasm of pleasure jerked from her body and pulsed from his, she looked up, into the eyes of...

"*DAVID!*"

Her shrill outburst instantly broke her husband's hypnotic trance, unconsciously angering him even more.

Shoving Jennifer roughly aside, the man on the bed looked up to meet David's cold, piercing eyes. All sexual desire was gone from him. Now, discovered, his only thought was of escape. But, how? The window led to a long drop. And the bitch's husband blocked the only other exit.

The three of them stood gazing at one another in silence. The fetid smell which David had first noticed still hung, permeating the air. As the odor filtered into his nostrils again, his mind snapped, and all hell broke loose.

He leaped across the room, bringing his large, powerful hand down alongside Jennifer's blushed face.

"YOU BITCH! YOU DAMNED BITCH! I'LL BEAT THE SHIT OUT OF YOU!"

In his rage, David did not notice the stranger ease from the bed, nor did he notice the crashing tinkle of breaking glass behind him.

Again, his fist struck out. This time the blow caught Jennifer just under the left jaw, knocking her from the bed onto the cool marble floor.

"I'm not finished with you!" David panted, his feet tangling with the clothing on the floor as he moved closer to his wife. Suddenly, there was a sharp pain in the center of his back. His mouth distorted, and his teeth clamped together tightly. He felt the need to scream, but forcefully suppressed it. His mind instantly flashed the panorama of events before him.

The stranger?

The vague remembrance of a crash. *Glass? A bottle? Yes, the room stunk of whiskey.* The bastard had broken a bottle over the marble-topped night stand.

David, in his discomfort, was angered at his own stupidity. He had completely forgotten Jennifer's lover. Now he was paying for his oversight.

"You son-of-a-bitch!" The words were meant more for himself than his attacker. Blood soaked the back of his white shirt where the jagged edges of the broken bottle had been jammed into his back and twisted. The circular jagged edge of the bottle sliced through his skin ripping muscle, tissue, and veins. Blood rushed from the ragged wound.

In the rapid chain of events the attacker had sobered quickly. Instinctively he sought to protect the woman who had made love to him. Now, after his initial attack, however, his only thought was to escape.

If he could get to the Fiat Spider outside, he would be free, leaving this scene of insanity behind him forever. He wouldn't bother dressing. Take too much time. He could dress in the car. Just get the hell out!

David Jeffrey turned in time to see the attacker-lover rush out the door. He heard him stumble down the stairs, utter a cry of pain, heard him stumble again, then heard the sound of the front door opening. The attacker did not bother to close the door as he rushed into the humid summer night. He was free.

David turned, staring at his wife. She had not screamed during the attack, as he thought she might have. In fact, it appeared to have had the completely opposite effect on her. She was laughing at him, drunk and hysterical. The sight of his distress amused her to no end.

His pain turned and again for the second time in but a few minutes he knew rage. He said quietly, "Your friend got away, but I'm not forgetting you!"

Jennifer laughed, her drunken words slurring together. "Yes-you-are-you-bastard!" Her eyes were glazed with long hidden insanity.

(2)

Angelica sat erect in the twin brass bed, her feet tucked under the cool cotton sheets. She had awakened from a dream, trembling. Even with mussed hair and sleep-filled eyes, she was an attractive girl. In her half-dream state, the strange events of the evening had been forgotten.

The room was exceptionally dark. On the night table a clock ticked loudly. It was 1:32 a.m. The girl scanned the room, her pupils dilated just enough to make out familiar objects: the white Fantona book shelf; the Naples American High School pennant; and the large inlaid-wood jewelry box her father had given her five months ago when she had celebrated her entrance into her senior year in high school. Everything seemed to be in place. It had only been a dream. She lay back, quietly, pulling the sheet up around her chin. The trembling, however, persisted. Memories of the voices in the cave began to come back, despite her efforts to fight them.

From the outer room came the sound of movement. Daddy. He's always prowling around in the middle of the night, she thought. Ever since she could remember, he had worked into the wee hours of the morning. He was always working it seemed.

There were times, however, that he did find a few moments to relax. At those times he and Angelica laughed, played, and grew together. She loved baking for him or surprising him with tea or coffee while he labored over a new book. He loved her too. She was sure of that.

Content that the noise had been made by her father, Angelica's eyes closed. But she could not sleep. Her head was filled with the chanting voices.

The soul cannot die. It will survive forever. The soul cannot die. It will live for...

"DAVID!"

Through the chanting came the sound of her mother's scream. What had happened? She was scared, motionless. The lifeless quiet of a tomb filled the room. First the voices and now her mother crying out.

Angelica wanted to pull the sheet over her head and feel protected, as she had when she was a baby. Instead, she stepped from her bed. Even though her room was one of the few in the house with the luxury of carpeting, she instinctively slid her feet into a pair of beige house slippers.

Something was wrong. From upstairs, her father's voice now filled the air with obscenities. An argument? She had never known her parents fight, or even exchange words of anger.

She timidly peered out, wanting to listen, but afraid of what she might hear. The upstairs bedroom was dimly illuminated. The door was slightly open. She could hear the crash of something breaking. Glass. Though not distinct enough to make out, she could see a figure moving inside the bedroom. What was happening? What was wrong? She trembled, a cold tingle running down her spine. The angered cries had ceased with the sound of the smashing glass.

"You son-of-a-bitch!" It was her father. He was up there. But who was he yelling at? Her mother? Why?

The figure again. A scream. Someone rushed into the upstairs hall! A man! She had never seen him before. He was tall, thin, and... naked! She could clearly see his mature loins covered with pubic hair.

What was wrong? Tears began to trickle from her eyes.

She closed the door slightly. From behind the tiny opening, everything - including the stranger on the upstairs landing - could be viewed perfectly. A bundle of clothes was clutched in his arms. He began descending the stairs, missing every other step.

Angelica felt herself shaking. Her thin nightgown was soaked with perspiration. The tips of her blond hair clung to the moist material. The man was getting closer.

The sound of heavy breathing filled the room. It was her own breathing, echoing.

The man had gotten about halfway down the stairs when he fell.

Things were happening too rapidly, with no explanations to divide them, set them in order. Angelica wanted to scream, call for her parents. But instead, she cried harder.

"SHIT!" The sound ripped the silence. As the man tumbled, his face struck the corner of a step, blood pouring from his chin.

Angelica closed her eyes tightly. This had to be a dream.

"Please God, it has to be a dream." Her whispers were stuttered. She was weeping now, scared, trembling. What was going on? And who was this strange man?

In his agony and desire to escape, Jennifer's lover did not notice the sounds coming from Angelica's room, as he had the first time.

She heard the front door open. Her eyes widened as she peered out the crack. There was no one.

The house appeared empty. If not for the opened front door, Angelica might have actually believed it had been a dream, conceived from within some unknown chamber of her unconscious mind. But the door was open. And heavy sounds once again flowed down to her from the master bedroom. They were too faint to make out, but Angelica was certain it was the voice of her mother.

(3)

Like a giant cat, Jennifer sprang from the corner, pouncing upon her husband's pain-ridden body. Suddenly, she had become the aggressor - biting, scratching and kicking. And all the while, belching a psychotic laugh. For her size, she seemed to possess superhuman strength.

David was pinned beneath her. Pieces of the broken bottle still protruded from his back, leaving him unable to defend himself completely. If he remained in his present position, though, it would be only a matter of time before Jennifer bashed his skull to bits on the slick marble floor.

Though she was in a state of shock, perhaps he could reason with her.

"Jennifer." His voice came out soft but firm. "Jennifer, it's me, David."

The sudden change frightened her. Where was she? Who was she? Leaping from her husband's back, she scurried into the dark corner. Chills rushed through her naked body. She was shaking, unable to control the movements. Trickles of sweat flowed over her glistened skin. Tears welled in her eyes.

David struggled to his feet and managed to remove the jagged glass from his back. He had broken Jennifer's insane trance. She now recognized him, he thought.

"Jennifer? Oh!" Sharp, rippling pains pierced his back where the bottle had penetrated. He was hurt. But he must first consider Jennifer's safety. "Ohhhhh!" He eased forward, the pain growing. "Jennifer, oh Jennifer. I'm sorry. I'm so sorry. Come here, sweetheart. Come to me." David's arms were extended towards his wife. She was crying. She needed him. In his agony, though, he needed her even more.

"What do you want from me?" she growled in response.

"Jennifer, it's all right. It's me, David."

"David?"

"Honey, you're all right. Just come... oh... come here to... to me."

"STAY AWAY!" She clawed at the air like an attacking eagle, or a trapped animal. David froze, trembling. A grin passed over Jennifer's face, indicating pleasure from his response.

Out of the corner of her eye she could see the reflection of a woman on the verge of insanity in the fractured wardrobe mirror. It had been broken, leaving only long, tooth-like slivers and knife-like shards. She did not remember her drunken lover falling against it earlier that evening. But she was enticed by the thin, angry-looking slivers of glass which glittered, scattered on the floor. Gazing at them, her mind began to play with thoughts of insanity. Ideas that, for centuries, have been hosted by murderers.

In the corner she found the knit blouse that had been randomly tossed aside earlier in the evening. She now wrapped the garment around her bare hand and slowly stood. Her protected hand swiftly snatched a jagged piece of glass from the broken dresser mirror.

He would not get her, of this she was sure.

In the low light he had not seen what his wife had done. He moved closer, still reaching.

SLASH! The long, thick piece of glass split his flesh cleanly, allowing blood to spray from David's throat. It occurred so fast that he was helpless. A gurgling sound of air and liquid, then he was breathless.

SLASH! Pain! David looked down. Intestines were spilling out of his gaping stomach. He gazed at his once loving wife with staring eyes.

She's killed me, was his last thought. His body fell hard, his skull cracking as it hit the marble floor. Blood spewed from the incisions, then eased into a foaming broth.

(4)

Angelica stood in the doorway, staring at the motionless figure on the floor. Dim light from the night stand fixture illuminated the body. It seemed as if it had taken hours to climb the stairs leading to her parent's bedroom. Now she saw no one. That is, no one alive.

"Daddy?"

Blood oozed from his slit throat. Foam seeped from the parted, blue lips. His green eyes now bulged, cold and gray. Hauntingly he seemed to beckon her. Trembling, she fell beside her father. His stomach had been savagely ripped, as if struck by an ax. Strings of intestine, covered in white mucus, bulged from the gash. The putrid odor of human excrement filled the room. The girl's lips moved without sound. Her chest heaved uncontrollably as she inhaled the polluting smell. Her sight blurred as tears filled her eyes.

"Daddy. DADDY!" The sound echoed through the room and returned to the echo chamber of her mind. Then, once again, silence engulfed the room. Her unsteady hand stretched towards the body. It was not stiff or cold as she had expected. It felt warm and pleasant to the touch.

"Daddy?" Her voice no longer contained the tone of fear, but rather, the soft whisper of a child. She shifted, placing her father's head on her lap. Her fingers, soaked with blood, slowly caressed the broken skull.

"ANGELICA!"

Through the darkness she could see her mother's eyes. She had been hunched in the corner. Waiting for her.

"ANGELICA! Come here to Mamma! What have you done to Daddy? WHAT HAVE YOU DONE?"

"No, Mamma. I didn't do anything," Angelica sobbed.

"HE'S DEAD! DEAD! And you killed him, Angelica! You killed your daddy! He loved you, and you killed him!"

"No, Mamma, I didn't do anything. Mamma, no." Tears flowed down her face as she spoke. Her mind reeled with confusion. Did she actually kill her father? Was her mother telling the truth? So much had happened so quickly that she could no longer conceive what had actually taken place. The strange man running out of the house, her parents arguing, the screams and the hideous laughter. Now, somehow, she was no longer in the safety of her own room. She was in her mother's bedroom - her father dead in her arms.

"He always loved you more than he did me. You and that damn writing. I didn't want much. But you had to have him all to yourself. You couldn't share him with me. Whenever he wasn't working, you hoarded him from me. So I found some-one. And I liked it. I like having someone to love. Someone to give me love. And you told him. You told him, didn't you? That's why he's dead. You killed him. You KILLED HIM! MURDERER! LOOK AT THE BLOOD ON YOUR HANDS! MURDERER!"

"NO! No! No, no."

"I heard you Angelica. I heard you talking against me. You took him from me. And then you told him about my lover. I heard you! You made him hate me!"

"No, Mother. I never said anything against you. Mother, I love you. Mother...."

A silence filled the room, broken only by the rhythmic breathing of mother and daughter. Their eyes remained fixed on each other. Waiting. A dog-like growl came from the dark corner, where her mother crouched. Angelica slowly lifted her father's head from her lap. A plopping sound broke the stillness as the head dropped into the pool of blood. The girl crawled across the room to escape her mother's evil eyes.

"Come here, Angelica. I'll show you what happens to little girls who talk against their mothers. I'll show you. Come here. COME HERE!"

Angelica watched her mother ease out of the corner. She had been unable to see the full figure of the woman in the darkness, but now, as she stepped into the light, the terrified girl noticed the older woman's nakedness. Glistening red blood oozed from her left breast, trickling over her firm stomach and onto her pubic hair. The jagged glass, still dripping from the fresh kill, rested in her right hand.

"Mamma's going to show you what happens to girls who have a wagging tongue. You told Daddy, didn't you? You told him. Well, my dear, you won't tell anyone else. Not with that wagging tongue.

Come here to Mamma."

Flexing her right hand, she prepared the deadly weapon. One foot raised and moved closer to the girl, followed by the other. Her freed breasts rising and falling in rhythm with her breathing.

"I'll get that wagging tongue of yours."

It had seemed the right thing to do when Angelica crawled to the opposite side of the room to huddle into the corner. Now, however, she realized that she had cut off any chance of escape. Her mother blocked the only exit. A mixture of perspiration and tears dripped from the girl's chin, leaving a cold chill as it ran into her opened nightgown and down her chest. It was as if she were caught in a nightmarish dream. She expected to wake at any moment, but as the older woman, in her blood-hungry lust, came closer, the moment of awakening salvation never came. She was not sleeping. And now her mother, only steps away, wanted to kill her, like she had killed her father. She was crazy.

Angelica felt a hard, powerful hand clench her throat. She was in shock. Resistance did not even occur to her. Under the vice-like pressure, her mouth opened, causing her tongue to slide between her parted lips.

An insane laugh came from the possessed woman. "There it is! Yes. That's it. A little farther. There! Ahhhhhh, ahhh-hhh!" The bloody glass swooped through the air.

Pain seared through the girl. A flood of hot blood filled her mouth and gushed out. The last thing she saw was a silhouette of her mother, laughing. Like an infant, she tried to call to her for comfort. But words could no longer be formed in her mouth.

Then, Angelica again heard the voice... "*The soul cannot die. It will survive forever,*"...before everything went black.

From the Sunday edition of the *International Herald Tribune.*

AMERICAN AUTHOR AND DAUGHTER DIE IN GAS EXPLOSION

Naples, Italy: American author David Jeffrey, 38, and his daughter Angelica, 13, died in their southern Italian home last Friday as a result of a gas explosion, according to officials of the Naples police who investigated the accident.

The explosion took place at approximately 5:20 a.m., Inspector Angelo di Cicco told reporters, when Jeffrey entered the kitchen and turned on a light, causing a spark which triggered the blast. Investigators concluded that gas had apparently leaked from the kitchen's bottled gas canister, causing the explosion.

"Explosions of this type," di Cicco stated, "are fairly common in Italy. Jeffrey was utilizing a larger than normal gas bottle, therefore resulting in greater damage, as well as a fire."

Jeffrey, who was killed instantly according to medical reports, had lived in Italy for the past fourteen years. He was author of several best-selling books, including Death in the Mafia *and* A Touch of Murder. *His novel* Velvet Dagger *won him the National Book Award for fiction as well as the Crime Writers' Association's Golden Dagger Award.*

Angelica Jeffrey, a student at the Naples American High School, was sleeping in the room next to the kitchen when the explosion took place and was trapped when fire broke out, engulfing the entire first floor of the villa. The girl's right arm and hand were the only remains found.

Jennifer Jeffrey, 35, was asleep in an upstairs bedroom at the time of the accident. Reports say that she jumped from the window, suffering only minor cuts, bruises, and shock. She was treated at the First Policlinic of the University of Naples.

JEFFREYS

Owosso, Michigan

(1)

The sun shone brightly on Lexington Avenue. Rebecca Jeffrey stood staring out at two tiny squirrels through the sliding glass patio doors. It was 8:05 a.m. But there was no need to rush. She would not be going to school this morning. This was the day of her appointment. Her mother would drive her to East Main Street, there would be a fifteen minute wait, finally Doctor Beaumont would open his door and ask her to step in and sit on the couch. Then, he would proceed to pump questions at her. It was always the same. Still, Becky didn't mind. It kept her out of school for a while.

Valerie Jeffrey was in the kitchen preparing pancakes and sausage for her family. She had a busy day ahead of her. Today was wash day. Becky had to be at the doctor's office at eleven - the dry-cleaning could be dropped off on the way - and there were groceries to buy. After lunch, she'd drop Becky off at school. She would only make the last two hours, but her father insisted that she go to American History class. He was probably right. She hadn't been doing as well this year as in the past. Then again, the problem had never been this severe before.

Walking into the adjacent dining area, Valerie placed the sausage on the table next to the pancakes, butter and maple syrup.

"The squirrels out this morning?" she asked, glancing towards her twelve-year-old daughter.

"Ah? Oh, yeah, there's two of 'em out there playin' with a bread wrapper."

"Come on honey, before the pancakes get cold. Jack, come and eat."

Jack Jeffrey applied the last handful of Rapid Shave to his face and began skimming it off with the Gillette Trac II. The hair pulled from the roots, leaving his face red and stinging. Bits of hair and soap from previous shaves had filled the space between the parallel blades. Unfortunately, it was the only one he had left. He couldn't go without shaving. Not with his job.

In college he had studied archeology with hopes of world travel and perhaps, someday, even a great discovery. Sir Arthur Evans had been his idol for years - a man who had come from nowhere to discover an ancient civilization and gain worldwide recognition. That's what he would do someday, he often told himself. But during his senior year all his hopes and ambitions were abandoned.

He met Valerie, a thin, dark-haired sophomore from Ohio, in front of Owen Hall. He remembered the day clearly and laughed to his reflection in the mirror. It had been snowing for days, leaving roads slick with patches of ice. Valerie had turned off Boquest Street onto East Shaw Lane in her parents' '64 Ford Maverick. He had just finished his last class of the day and was returning to the dormitory. She had not seen him step onto the street - or so she said - until it was too late to stop. As she turned sharply to the right, the car spun twice and landed in a three-foot snow drift. She was furious, insisting it had been his fault. He contested that he had right-of-way and that she should have been watching where she was going instead of daydreaming. After things had at least cooled down between them - and the car was back on the road - Jack had offered to buy her coffee. Thus, their relationship began.

Three months later, Valerie announced she was pregnant. At that time, the pill was something taken for a headache and abortions were performed by medical dropouts in back alley slums.

Besides, neither of them looked upon her pregnancy as a misfortune. They were in love. So - why shouldn't they be man and wife? As Valerie put it, they had moved from Step A to Step C and forgotten B. Two weeks later they exited the high arched dome of St. Anthony Chapel as Mr. and Mrs. Jack Jeffrey.

The unexpected events did, however, have an effect on Jack's career plans. Valerie had a miscarriage, which hit both of them hard. They struggled through the school year. Jack graduated. Then came considerations such as house, furniture, bills, and biggest of all, a job. They began searching the want ads of the neighboring cities - Lansing, Flint, Saginaw, Grand Rapids, Ann Arbor - and finally Jack landed a position with Metropolitan Life as an insurance agent. He despised the term salesman. And since he would be working out of the Flint office, a move was inevitable. They settled in the town of Owosso, 32 miles west of Flint. Both of them enjoyed the peace as well as the people.

Becky had been born nine years later in Memorial Hospital. Jack had moved up in the insurance field and was currently the top sales manager of Michigan. Valerie, meanwhile, proved to be an excellent wife and mother.

Jack smiled at himself as the last patch of white foam was removed. He hadn't done too badly. And he was happy.

"Jack! Your breakfast's getting cold."

Yes, she was a good wife all right.

"Okay, be right there."

He replaced the razor in its case, placed the can of shaving lather in the medicine cabinet, splashed his cheeks with Old Spice, and was ready for the day.

"Smells good," Jack said, looking down at his daughter who had already finished one heap of pancakes.

"It is," came Becky's muffled reply.

Valerie came in from the kitchen to the dining area holding a Corning ware coffee pot. It was part of a set Jack had given her last year for Christmas.

"Sit down...here's your coffee. Your pancakes are probably cold by now."

Jack took his place at the head of the table. "Becky, pass the sausages, please."

"Did you pay the electricity bill yet?" Valerie asked.

"I forgot, honey. I've been so busy breaking in the new man. I think he's going to be all right though. He made four sales on his own last week."

Valerie knew she should have taken care of the bill.

"Maybe he'll be all right, but if we don't get that bill paid, Consumers Power is going to be breathing down our necks."

"I'll take care of it." Jack hoped he'd have time.

"Give it to me. I'll stop at the payment window on the way to the doctor's office. Do you have the checkbook?"

"Yeah, it's in my blue sports jacket pocket." There was a pause of silence. "I didn't know you had a doctor's appointment today."

"Not me. Becky. She has to see Dr. Beaumont today. Why do you think she's not at school? I told you last week. You didn't forget about that too, did you? He wants both of us there this time."

Jack had a smile on his face. His years as an insurance salesman had taught him to use it to cover up any true emotion. He had forgotten. "Of course I remember...eleven o'clock, right?"

That means the new man will have to make the morning appointments alone, he thought. Cochran wouldn't like that.

It also meant a half hour drive to the office, a half hour back, another half hour return to Flint, and finally the drive home this evening. Just what he needed, two hours on the road...if there was no traffic. The Monte Carlo used so much gas, too.

"Okay, I'll meet you there at five to eleven," Jack said, smiling. "Sure he wanted both of us?"

"That's what he said, Jack."

He sighed. The smile was gone.

Becky had been silent through the discussion. Then she interrupted: "Wait, wait a minute - I'll settle it. Why don't we all stay home and forget Dr. Beaumont, work, and school?"

Jack and Valerie looked at each other, then at Becky, and all three began to laugh.

"All right," Jack finally broke in. "I'll see you both at the doctor's office. Now can I eat in peace?" He reached across the table, speared a stack of pancakes and slid them onto his plate. They were cold.

"These are cold."

"I'm gonna cold you," replied Valerie as she moved over to kiss her husband on the cheek. "You'd better get out of here or you'll be late."

He glanced down at his digital Seiko. "Geez, it's twenty to nine already! See you later sweetheart," he said, kissing his wife. He sprinted through the living room, slipped into the dark blue sports jacket, and was out the door.

Three minutes later, Jack Jeffrey was going east on Main Street, headed for Michigan's motor city. He had not heard Valerie calling out as he drove off. She had not gotten the checkbook. The electricity bill wouldn't get paid again today.

UNSEEN FRIENDS I

(1)

Valerie glanced at the sign as they walked towards the heavy frosted glass door. Dale Beaumont, MD, Psychiatry. This was not the first time she had seen the words. She had seen them many times in the two years they had been bringing their child here. They first brought Becky here for treatment two years ago, when she was just ten. Since then, it had been a monthly affair. So, she had seen that glass door at least twenty-four times. In reality though, thought Valerie, Dr. Beaumont had done little for her child. And despite repeated discussions, Jack persisted in continuing with the visits. Fortunately the insurance paid for Becky's visits.

The heat hit them as soon as they opened the door. It was the kind of stuffy, sweltering heat present when an air conditioner malfunctions. It was obvious that the air conditioner in the waiting room was out of order. Valerie recognized it instantly. She should. She had grown up in a home along the Gulf Coast without air conditioning. A woman slightly past middle-age, her hair wilted and sticking to her head, sat in one of the high-backed leather-clad chairs that lined one wall. She was fanning herself with a folded copy of last week's *Time*. On the opposite wall a large window-like opening, complete with sliding glass panes, had been cut out, giving access to the receptionist's office.

A rush of cold air rushed out and over Valerie as she pushed aside the glass pane on the left. It felt wonderful.

"Mrs. Jeffrey. The doctor will be right with you," said the young blonde girl behind the desk. She wore green fingernail polish with tiny gold flecks in it, and had the same kind of pointy white glasses that looked identical to the ones worn by Daryl Hanna in *Steel Magnolias*. The glasses were straight out of the 1950s.

The *Time* magazine suddenly stopped its swift left-right, right-left sweep, and the gray-haired woman, with the damp, plastered hair glared in their direction. Valerie noticed the woman had rivers of sweat rolling off her.

The receptionist's name was Wendy, and Valerie turned back to say, "How long's the AC been out?"

"Couple hours," said Wendy, glancing down at her parrot green nails. "The repairman was here, but had to go get a part. Don't know when he'll be back."

Valerie had been to the office enough times to know them all. This one was totally different from Linda and Betty, the other receptionists Dr. Beaumont had in the past. Wendy was tall, thin, and extremely good looking, despite the ugly glasses and the hideous-colored fingernail polish.

Valerie thought, *perhaps sexy would be a better term, rather than good looking*. Wendy also had billows of thick blond hair, looking as if she had just stepped from a shampoo ad. As a receptionist, she actually seemed a bit drifty, and Valerie couldn't help but wonder if maybe she didn't offer other services to the doctor?

She scolded herself mentally. She shouldn't be thinking such things.

Wendy might be a perfectly nice person. A little young, but still, perfectly nice. Still, it wasn't the first time the thought had crossed her mind about Dr. Beaumont's receptionists. Each of them had been extremely good looking with a body men could not help but notice. And Dr. Beaumont was far from being old. In fact, he was a tall, good looking, muscular man, with hair just turning salt and pepper. Valerie had even entertained her own fantasies about the two of them.

Becky fidgeted in the chair and Valerie thought that for an expensive chair, it must be the noisiest one in that part of the state. Every time Becky even wiggled, the legs would squeak, and the leather would make a groaning noise. The large-faced bronze and wooden clock on the wall across the room read two minutes to eleven. Becky noticed her father hadn't arrived, and knew her mother was growing angrier by the minute.

He was twenty-five minutes late when he got there, and he looked as if he had already been sitting in the hot room for a half hour. His collar was open at the neck and his tie was pulled down a couple of inches. It was 11:25 when Jack arrived and Becky had been right, her mother was, by now, furious. The waiting room was even hotter than when they had arrived, and not-so-small rivulets of sweat had been on a sojourn down both her shoulder blades, while another steady stream trickled between her breasts. She was miserable and reminded of those long hot summers in Mobile. Valerie was waving, with one hand, a copy of *Vogue Magazine* in the same cadence as the *Time Magazine* across the room, and she drummed the fingers of her other hand over her suede leather purse. She wasn't just angry, she was pissed.

Becky had already been in with Doctor Beaumont twenty minutes and, unusually for Jack, he was late.

"Hi, honey. Sorry I'm late."

She did not respond, only stared straight ahead, the *Vogue* never faltered in its back and forth swing.

"We had a 9:30 appointment in Flushing," Jack explained, trying to justify his late arrival. "Then we had to go all the way back to the office." He could see from her expression that any excuse he gave wouldn't be good enough, and he, vaguely, understood how she felt. There was only one thing that *he* hated more than late arrivals; that was being stood up. In his business he had plenty of both.

There was an uneasy rubbing groan from the leather seat as he settled in beside his wife. It was the same chair Becky had been sitting in.

"How long's she been in there?"

The tension seemed to ease some, and for that, he was relieved.

"Ten, fifteen minutes."

"Hot in here, isn't it?" There was no reply. Valerie stared ahead in stony silence.

"Did you wait long?"

Instantly he knew that he said the wrong thing. The words seemed to come out naturally enough, but he knew what was coming.

Anger erupted across her face, and she said sarcastically, "Not *nearly* as long as I did for you!"

"Come on, honey."

"I'll meet you there at five to eleven," she mimicked his earlier promise as if she were a girl younger than Becky, and with the same twist of the head a child would use on the playground at school.

"All right, so I'm late," he said icily. "A *little* late. I said I was sorry. What the *hell* do you want? What do you want me to do, get on my hands and knees and beg forgiveness?" he hissed. "I was less than thirty minutes late. Where were you going anyway?"

He was right. But still, she had felt ignored. Felt as if she hadn't mattered. After all, it was him that wanted Becky to continue seeing the doctor.

It angered her. If he *thought* that all she had to do was sit around a doctor's office all day, he was wrong. But, wrong or not, she did still love *him*...and love their daughter.

"Maybe you're right. But I seldom ask you to go out of your way to do anything. Then when I do need you, you can't even show up on time. I'm always the one that has to bring Becky. She's your daughter too." She had turned to face him directly. Her face was wet with perspiration, and her hair, like the woman's sitting across from them, was now wilted and plastered to her head. Her pastel yellow blouse with tiny white lace trim stuck to her.

"And I've got other things to do - buy groceries, make dinner, pay the bills *you* forgot..."

Jack lifted his hands and waved them in the air, frustrated. He preferred her silence. Slowly they gazed into each other's eyes. Then he leaned forward and kissed her, softly, tenderly. Valerie turned away to hide her smile, but he had seen it and tapped her on the shoulder.

"What?" she asked with a smile, then added, "You did forget to leave the checkbook this morning," she said.

(2)

Dale Beaumont leaned back in the large leather recliner, scribbled into a steno-notebook, then stretched. This was his most interesting and frustrating case. He had been with this girl two years. Two slow, relatively unsuccessful years. Her parents, so they said, had hopes for her recovering and becoming a normal child. And there was only one time they missed an appointment, if his memory was correct.

In his early career, he swore never to give up on a case, any case. But there were times, however, with this one, when he saw no possible hope. To be sure, Becky could live - to all outward appearances - a normal life. It was not as if she were dangerous. It was just her imagination.

"How are things, Becky?"

"Good, Doctor Beaumont. Real good." The girl was livelier than usual.

"You seem happy."

"I didn't have to go to school this morning," she smiled. "When I come to see you - in the mornings - I only have to go to school for the last two hours. But that includes history - and I hate *history* most of all." She made the word sound like something evil or dirty. He made another notation on the steno pad.

He leaned closer to the girl and smiled. "Well, just between you and me, we can schedule your appointments in the afternoon. I never liked history either."

"Not *too* late though. Then I'd have to go to morning classes."

"Okay, not too late. Not too early." He suddenly thought, *maybe that's why I continue to see her. She's young, and for the most part, she's happy, and... and she trusts me.* They had actually become friends. Her visits always left him with a good feeling. Unwittingly, she was *his* therapy.

There are three categories of mental illness: psychoses, neuroses, and personality disorders, Dale Beaumont recalled from his studies at the University of Michigan. He knew that some personality disorders could result from genetic make-up, faulty brain development, injury, infection, chemical effects, or what was commonly referred to as environmental factors. In the case of Becky Jeffreys, her problem was part of the latter. More specifically, it was the result of a traumatic childhood experience.

At the age of five, Becky, like hundreds of thousands of other kindergarten-aged children, began attending school for a half-day. She would catch the bus in front of her house at 11:30 in the morning and return on the same bus at 3 p.m.

She enjoyed everything about school: her teacher, her new friends, the school itself, but in particular, she enjoyed painting. Nearly every day she'd bring home splashes of watercolor on heavy, multi-colored paper.

"That's nice," her mother would say. "Is that Daddy?" Becky would giggle at this, gaze up, and say: "Mom, that's Joker. Don't you see his tail?"

Valerie could not help but laugh, too, at the thought that she had confused their dog, Joker, for her husband, Jack, although in her daughter's picture they did look similar.

As the seasons changed, so did Becky's artwork. Snow began to play a major role in her youthful art and soon Christmas would be the main theme. There were only three weeks before the holiday break, and Becky was looking forward to it for two reasons. First, she loved getting presents.

Second, Mr. Kelso, her regular bus-driver, had begun his vacation on Monday and Becky did not like his replacement.

"Now, you kids sit down and keep your mouths closed!" The gray-haired man shouted. "I don't want to hear a peep."

For the past two days, the twenty-minute ride to and from school had been filled with fear and silence. This afternoon was no exception. Becky walked to the back of the bus and sat in the next to last seat on the right.

The brown, plastic-covered seat was hard, almost frozen from the sub-zero winter temperature. Below the seat, however, hot air blew from the bus heater. To get warm, Becky lay across the seat, dangling her hands to catch the warm air. It had been a rough day in Mrs. Bagley's kindergarten class.

Five minutes later, Becky Jeffreys was fast asleep. She would sleep for nearly five hours. When she finally awoke, the five-year-old was cold. It was dark and she was alone in the back of a locked bus.

"How is Gary?" Doctor Beaumont asked.

"Not bad. We were just talking yesterday. Susan was there too."

It was the same story. Always the same. After two years, he had made little progress. That is, until their last session. He had been gazing out the window thinking about the upcoming weekend and his new thirty-foot sailboat.

Without thinking, he asked, "Did you go out with your friends this week?"

"They can't go out, Doctor Beaumont, you know that. You know, last week Susan told me that if she stepped one foot out of our yard the truant officer would be there in a second to take her to reform school. I told you that. Don't you remember?"

He did not remember. But what she had said began to turn in his mind. Perhaps this was the missing key.

Jack and Valerie Jeffreys had sought medical help for their daughter four years after the girl's traumatic experience in the bus. After hours of searching, the Shawassee County Police had located the lost girl locked in Bus 21 in the Owosso School District parking lot. She had been there nearly nine hours.

Becky did not return to school that year. She became isolated, spending hours in her room, seemingly playing by herself. One afternoon, however, Valerie overheard her daughter talking.

"Of course we'll have lunch together...What? Sure, Susan you're invited too."

Opening the door to the child's room, Valerie asked, "Are you playing house, honey?"

"Yeah, Mom. Susan and Gary are going to have lunch with me."

"That's fine," she replied, giving little concern to Becky's unseen playmates. She too had had imaginary friends during her youth. Five years later, however, when their daughter still insisted on talking to the unseen Susan and Gary, there was cause for major concern.

The Jeffreys other preoccupation was that of getting Becky to return to school the year after she had been locked in the bus. They had used several tactics - gifts, driving her each day so that she would not have to take the bus, even spending time at school with her. The thing that seemed to impress the girl, though, was Jack's discussion of how a truant officer roams the city looking for kids that are supposed to be in school but do not go.

"And if he catches you, you'll be put into reform school. That's like being in prison." He had said it in a joking manner.

His words, however, filled Becky's nightmares for months afterwards.

Dale Beaumont had linked the girl's subconscious fear of the truant officer and her imaginary friends. But he had never really considered the theory of disassociation through the physical restrictions Becky had placed on Gary and Susan. That is, until their last session.

"What did you say?" The words seemed to pass like pictures in his mind, triggering something out of his early graduate training.

"What, Doctor Beaumont?" His excitement had startled her.

"What you said before, honey." His voice was calm this time. However, inside nervous tension was building.

"I said: don't you remember?"

"No, no. Before that. What Susan told *you*?"

"She said that if she stepped out of the yard the truant officer would get her."

"Gary, too?"

"I guess so."

That is what he wanted to hear. The key. He had listened to her talk of these two imaginary friends for twenty-four months, knew that they - at least in her mind - could not leave the Jeffreys' home. Still, until now, he had never pondered that as a major point. Now, perhaps he had finally come up with the hidden piece of the puzzle. A chance? Yes, but even a chance in this case would be a breakthrough.

"Becky, what would happen if you never went to school?"

"But I do go to school, except when I'm sick or have an appointment with you. Even then I have to take a note." The girl seemed uneasy. "I don't skip, really."

"I know you don't. I didn't mean *you* skipped. I was just wondering what happens to kids who *do* skip school."

"They get picked up by the truant officer. Then they're taken to reform school. Those places are full of big rats." She shivered instinctively. "I hate rats! So does Susan."

The puzzle was falling into place. She had taken the stories of her father and her imagination and had added to them until, in her mind, reform school had become a place of Medieval torture.

"Does anything else happen to kids that get picked up by the truant officer?" Dale Beaumont was probing. At last he felt as if they were progressing, and it excited him.

"Sure. Did you know that they are beaten?"

(3)

It was 12:45 when Doctor Beaumont and Becky emerged from the tiny room. Jack had become worried. They had never gone over the one hour limit before. Beaumont had wanted to confirm his theories again before talking to the girl's parents.

"Afternoon, Jack," the psychiatrist reached out his hand. The girl's father returned the gesture. "Sorry about the air conditioning." He waved a well-manicured hand in the air, indicating the room where they stood.

"Why so long this time?" Jack didn't mention the lack of air conditioning, though he was obviously hot, sweat-stained under both arms and his back was completely soaked.

"This time," the doctor grinned. "How do you know how long our meetings are? You're never here."

Valerie looked up, first at the doctor, then her husband.

"Don't you start too, Dale. I've already been through that with her." The three of them smiled for a moment and then a tone of seriousness came across Jack's face.

"Nothing still?" he whispered.

Beaumont looked at both parents. "Becky, wait here for a minute, I want to talk to your mom and dad."

"Okay, Doctor Beaumont."

Sweeping his hand towards the back office, the doctor led the Jeffreys down the long corridor. The blast of cold air brought near instant relief.

Once in the office, he turned to them. "I think we've made progress. In fact, if my theory is correct, we should be able to take care of our "problem girl" in a matter of months, maybe weeks."

Valerie was speechless. After two years, only a matter of weeks, months? She wanted to ask, but Jack spoke first.

"What is it?"

"Well, like I said, if I am right, it is very simple. In fact, perhaps it's too simple. Maybe that's why it has taken so long. In cases such as this you're always looking for a hidden malfunction. A mental disorder of some type. In Becky's case, I think it's a matter of conditioning and unacceptance, beyond the trauma she experienced.

"Look at your daughter. Most girls her age are involved in a variety of activities, beginning to have friends of the opposite sex as well as a number of companions in the same sex group. Becky has none of these. Because of the trauma she experienced in her early childhood, Becky was different than other kids. In turn, she has been rejected by her peers and she has grown to dislike school."

Valerie could take no more, "But what does that have to do with these...these invisible people?"

"No!" Doctor Beaumont burst out in excitement of his discovery, as if it was obvious to everyone.

"They are not people, they are her friends. Her only true friends. You see, when she became rejected in school, she maintained the playmates she created during her hours alone on the bus. This is not uncommon in young children. With Becky, though, these imaginary friends further hindered her chances of making real ones. I recall about a year ago, she mentioned a girl at school who, it seemed, wanted to become a friend. Once Rebecca mentioned her fantasized friends, however, the girl categorized your daughter as being abnormal. This has been the case throughout Becky's school years. As a result, she no longer seeks peer companionship.

Jack could feel the perspiration still trickling from his underarms, but he was getting cooler. Twenty-four hours protection, what a joke. He wished Beaumont would come out with the meat and cut the psychiatric synopsis. He was self-conscious of his odor, his deodorant having failed long ago.

"So where does all this leave us, Dale?"

"I think the key is your house. Her so-called friends, according to her, cannot leave your property." Dale Beaumont leaned back and rocked in the chair. He was proud of himself.

"How long has it been since you had a vacation?"

"Last summer," Valerie replied.

"Where did you go?"

"Ludington, spent a week in the State Park by Lake Hamland. Why?"

He didn't answer Valerie right away and Jack was getting impatient.

"Do you remember if Becky had any problems there? Did she talk or seem to play with any of her imaginary friends?"

"No, not that I recall."

He jumped like a schoolboy who didn't do his homework.

"Huh? Oh, no. No. I don't think so. She spent most of her time with us swimming and fishing. You know, the usual vacation things." He pushed his arms closer to his sides, hoping to conceal the body odor.

"I think Becky needs to get away from the house for a while.

If my theory is right, she will also leave behind her unseen friends. This will allow a disassociation period, and the more she is without her imaginary friends, the easier it will be for us to resolve her problem completely. Maybe a long vacation would do you all some good, hey Jack?"

(4)

"What do you think?" Valerie asked her husband as they walked out of the doctor's office.

"I think we need to think about it."

"You know what I'm thinking?"

Becky was already climbing into the car.

"No, what do you think?" he asked.

"I think this might be the perfect time to visit your sister-in-law. We've been talking about it for...what, eight years?"

Jack liked the idea, but needed time to see if it would work into his schedule. Things were getting hectic in the office.

"Let's talk about it later."

Reaching the car, Valerie leaned towards her husband. "Know what else I think?"

"No, what?"

"That you need to give me a kiss."

Their lips met, their earlier tension forgotten.

"Buckle up, honey," Valerie said to Becky. "See you tonight, sweetheart."

Jack walked to his own car, "We'll talk about the trip then," he said.

With that, Valerie backed the Buick Riviera out of the parking spot and drove off. She had gone only one mile when a thought crossed her mind: I forgot the checkbook. That electricity bill is never going to get paid.

DISTANT
CORRESPONDENCE

(I)

Jack had not written to his sister-in-law in years. Then again, she was not what one would call a literary correspondent herself. She would scribble a few notes periodically asking him to check on Social Security and VA benefits. Since the accident, she had taken care not to overlook anything due her.

"David had always been one for getting everything he had coming to him, whether from the military or a publisher. I'm sure he would want me to do the same."

These had been her parting words to Jack as he left the funeral. When the American Consulate in Naples contacted him with the news of the fire, he had immediately caught a TWA flight out of Detroit, making a Rome connection in New York. Time was essential, he realized, since bodies were not embalmed in Italy and funerals took place within one or two days of a death. David had once told him that.

In Naples, however, it was obvious there was no need to rush to bid his brother farewell. Even if there had been a professional embalming services, the fire had eliminated the need. After all, how does one embalm bones, he had thought? The body had been identified by David's wedding band and dental work. Investigators had come to the conclusion that

Jack's niece, Angelica, had been consumed in the blaze as well, perhaps caught under one of the heavy, wooden support beams which had fallen. The fire had begun in the kitchen of the ancient villa and police were still investigating the cause when Jack returned to the U.S.

"Finished?" Valerie's voice interrupted Jack's hypnotic recollection. He could hardly hear what she had said over the blaring television theme song of an *E.R.* re-run.

"What?"

"Are you finished?"

"Yeah. Do we have any airmail envelopes?"

"I don't know. Maybe there's some downstairs."

"Run down and look through the desk, will you?"

Valerie was staring at the television screen.

"Becky, go downstairs and get your father an envelope." She did not move. Like her mother, her eyes were fixed on the television picture.

"Don't knock yourselves out ladies, I'll go myself." Jack could have become angered and thrown a fit. But he knew it wouldn't change things any - at least not for the next thirty minutes - or until the next commercial.

Two hours passed before he eventually found what he was after. Becky had gone to bed and Valerie sat at the kitchen table reviewing the letter while Jack jotted the address on the red, white and blue bordered airmail envelope: Mrs. Jennifer Jeffrey, 14/A, Via Roma, Baia (NA) ITALY.

"What do you think?"

"I don't know - why not? She has plenty of room. And how many times has she asked us to visit?"

"That was before the fire, though. If you remember, it was your brother that invited us, not Jenny."

Jack folded the letter in an attempt to get it into the tiny envelope.

"If I know Jenny, she'll be happy to have us around. She never liked being alone."

"I feel sorry for her," Valerie said, wrapping an index finger around a few hanging strands of hair. It was a bad habit she had picked up in grade school and never lost. "If anything ever happened to you and Becky, I'd die." She eased her chair next to Jack's and placed her arm around his neck. Their conversation ceased momentarily, her last words turning over in their minds.

Jack stared into his wife's brown eyes. He loved her. Needed her. It was probably him that would suffer most should anything happen to his family. He had grown dependent on their support, their love, their presence. It was a secure feeling. And he knew his wife felt it also.

He moved his head downwards, meeting Valerie's warm lips. Slowly, tenderly, they removed each other's clothes, their bodies excited from their sensuous touching as they eased to the plush, green carpeting. There, they enjoyed each other's pleasures.

The next morning, Jack woke with an aching back and the beginning of a cold.

"Shouldn't have been playing in your birthday suit last night," Valerie grinned.

"Birthday suit, my ass," he whispered, not wanting Becky to hear. "I got it from that stupid Bill Thompson. All last week he sat at his desk hacking. When he talks to you he'll cough right in your face. I don't know how he sells as much as he does."

"Jealous?"

"Me? You'd better believe it."

The chrome toaster, which had been a wedding gift from Valerie's cousin, popped two slices of golden bread into the air, startling them both. Jack grabbed the toast, spread a blob of Gold Bonnet over the top, and took a bite as he headed for the door.

"The letter!"

"Oh shit. I'd forget my head if it wasn't attached."

Valerie handed him the tiny envelope. "And a kiss for your wife?"

NIGHTLY VISIONS

(1)

Valerie could feel herself moving downwards, though she could not see the steps. It was as if an ectoplasm-like mist surrounded her feet. A heavy wooden door blocked her path.

It's locked, she thought, retrieving a worn, silver skeleton key from the red apron. Red apron? This isn't mine. But whose was it? And why was she wearing it?

The questions passed as rapidly as they had come. She was there for a reason. And the reason was behind the door. Magically the key slipped into its proper place as if greased. It twisted and then disappeared when the door mysteriously eased open. An odor of stagnant humidity filtered out of the dark, damp, pit that awaited her. In the mildew her feet slid forward, down the steps.

Click!

Valerie's mind reeled. Her heart throbbed like a base drum.

A feeble glow of light seeped from a tiny overhead light at the far end of the room.

"Only the light switch," she whispered to herself, not concerned with the fact that it had switched itself on.

"Tomatoes. That's what I'm here for. Tomatoes."

"TOMATOES! Tomatoes! TOMATOES! Tomatoes..!"
The reverberating voices were feminine. Then masculine!
Feminine! Masculine!

"What do you want?!" The words did not come from
Valerie's mouth, but rather were shot at the unknown enemy
with the force of a telepathic bullet fired from a rifle. She had
hit the target. And, the voices began to fade.

"Tomatoooooooooes."

Then, there were glistening bottles of ripe tomato sauce
in front of her. She had found her goal. But, as her trembling
hands reached towards the long, thin bottle necks...

"Beware the eyes!"

Valerie froze. She trembled with terror. A pricking chill,
like a spider crawling up one's bare back, tickled, then quickly
eased through her. The voice was soft, childish, but at the
same time, hideous.

"Beware the eyes!" Again came the snake-like hiss.

"Beware the eyes! Beware the eyes! BEWARE THE
EYES! BEWARE THE EYES!" The voice now belched hate-
filled screams that seemed to come from the bowels of hell.
With each word, an air of putrid odor rushed past Valerie with
the force of a hurricane.

Suddenly, silence. A silence of death. A knowing silence.
Knowing that someone or something was lurking. Watching.
Listening. A knowing that one is not alone. The silence one
finds at midnight in a graveyard.

A foot step!

The air around Valerie was consumed by the stench. A
damp fog had engulfed the room, all but a whirling tunnel
which led to the source of the demonic sounds.

A second step. Sliding. Echoing.

Valerie's eyes widened so that the pupils appeared like tiny islands surrounded by a sea of creamy white. Her dry, cracked lips curled back revealing the tightly clenched teeth, adding to her already ghostly appearance.

There was a face at the end of the tunnel!

Valerie's temple expanded with every heartbeat. Her breathing came out in shudders.

It was the face of a girl. An attractive girl. But there was something about it that spoiled its beauty. Valerie stared at the image trying to pick out its flaw when she noticed the girl's eyes were closed.

"What do you want?" The words were involuntarily mouthed by Valerie. She continued to stare, waiting for a reply.

The girl's mouth opened. A soft, sympathetic voice escaped, repeating the warning.

"Beware the eyes." At the sudden change, almost pleading, tone in the voice, Valerie confidently glanced away from the girl for a moment to investigate her surroundings. When her focus returned to the whirling tunnel, the attractive girl had gone. In her place, hovering two feet from Valerie, was a horrible distorted face, surrounded by long matted hair.

The creature opened its mouth revealing four rotting teeth in an otherwise toothless cavern. The smell of rot bellowed from the panting lips.

"BEWARE THE EYES! BEWARE THE EYES! BEWARE THE EYES..!" The words blasted out, hitting Valerie with the power of a ripping sleet storm, cutting her face and causing droplets of blood to trickle under her chin and down her soft neck. She could feel the vomit heaving with the suction of a plunger in and out of her stomach. Just as she was ready to retch the gagging, semi-digested mucus, a scream heaved from her throat.

"NOOOoooooo!"

(2)

"Valerie! Valerie!" Jack shook his wife. Her hair and night-gown were soaked with perspiration.

"Valerie! Wake up, honey! Wake up!"

Her eyes snapped open. Her chest heaved spasmodically. Tears eased down her face as she realized it had only been a dream.

Jack could feel his wife trembling in his arms.

"It's okay, baby. It was only a nightmare. It's okay."

She clung to him. "Oh Jack, it was horrible."

"Okay, it's over now. Close your eyes. I'm right here. Close your eyes," he whispered, trying to comfort her.

Eyes! Eyes? EYES! BEWARE THE EYES! Jack's words triggered a flashback of the dream in Valerie's mind. Suddenly, a recollection of the sickening odor vividly surrounded her.

"Let me go!" She screamed, breaking her husband's grip. She jumped from the bed, raced down the dark hall into the bathroom and vomited.

DISTANT
CORRESPONDENCE

(2)

It had been three months since Jack mailed the letter to his sister-in-law in Baia, asking if she could put him and his family up for a couple of weeks during their vacation to Italy. He hadn't expected the reply to take so long. School had let out a month ago and July was nearly over. If Jenny's letter didn't arrive shortly their plans would have to be dumped. He had thought of calling her, but after the accident she had never replaced the telephone.

It was a sunny Thursday afternoon, typical August weather in Michigan. Jack would not be home for another four hours. Valerie was hanging freshly washed clothes on the line in the back yard. Becky was enjoying the shade on the east side of the house, swinging in the five-year old hammock as she read a paperback of *Peanuts*. Becky smiled at the final cartoon in the book - Snoopy whipping his hand out with a big grin after Linus had coached him to, "Shake hands, boy."

Becky yawned, then closed her eyes, letting the book fall onto the brownish-green, semi-burnt grass. She hadn't slept well last night and now was the perfect time to catch up on a few missed dreams. She hadn't seen Susan or Gary for over a week. It was probably too hot for them to come out, even though they could now that school was over. School. Summer was almost finished and she would soon have to go back. She hated the thought and shrugged it off, concentrating on going to sleep.

A semi-dream state was just taking over the girl's conscious mind when the heavy, white U.S. Mail truck pulled up to the Jeffrey's mailbox. Becky, hearing the rumbling V-8 engine, sat up, rubbing her tired eyes. A surge of excitement raced through the girl. Her father had promised they'd take a trip to Europe if the letter from Aunt Jenny came in the next two weeks. Maybe today was the day.

"Becky, you goin' to get the mail?" Valerie had also heard the truck and was just as anxious as her daughter to discover if the distant correspondence had arrived.

"Yeah, I'll get it," replied the girl, rolling out of the hammock onto the ground.

As she reached the mailbox, the vehicle pulled away, leaving behind a smelly cloud of diesel fumes that reminded Becky of being caught behind a bus in heavy traffic. Inside were two letters. One was from the Pacesetter Bank and Trust. The other was a small airmail envelope with six funny looking postage stamps. The envelope was addressed to her father. There was no return name on the back, however. Turning the letter over, Becky read the return address that had been penned on the sealing flap: "14A, Via Roma, Baia, Italy."

"MOM! MOM!" She ran frantically, waving the letter.

"It's here! The letter's here!" In her excitement she dropped the bank statement in the paved driveway.

"Becky!" Her mother's voice sounded harsh as she stood at the corner of the house.

"What?"

Valerie smiled at her daughter. "You dropped a letter."

"Oh, I thought you were mad. The letter's here mom! The one from Aunt Jenny!"

Valerie took the letter and began opening it as Becky raced down the drive to retrieve the one she had lost.

"What's it say, Mom?"

"Give me time to get it out, will you?" She was excited about the reply, making it that much more difficult opening the flimsy, light blue envelope. Finally, she managed to pull the letter free from its envelope and began reading.

"What, Mom? Did she say OK? Mom?"

The girl's questions were unanswered for a few seconds, then a smile eased across her mother's face.

"She said OK, right? Right? Come on, Mom!!"

"We're going to Italy! We're going to It-a-ly!"

"All right!" Becky jumped up and down then, excited as her mother. It was like a dream come true for both of them.

"What did she say? Give me the letter."

Valerie pulled the letter upwards, avoiding the swooping grip of her daughter.

"Wait a minute. Let's go in the house. Then you can see it. If anyone sees us out here dancing round like a couple of nuts, what'll they think?"

"I don't care what they think, I wanna see the letter!"

"Come on, let's go inside. Besides, I want to call your father."

Once inside Becky plopped onto the brown tweed sofa and began reading the letter.

Dear Jack,

It was, to say the least, a pleasant surprise to hear from you after all this time. Yes, I have been well, but have been troubled with insomnia recently. The doctor has prescribed some pills, but they don't help much. I spend much of my night walking throughout the house. You know I still have dreams of that night when David died.

I will be happy to have you stay with me as long as you like. I can't wait to see Valerie once again and little Becky. Do you realize that I have never even seen my own niece! Please let me know when you will be arriving so that I can prepare the rooms and buy extra food. I don't eat as much as I used to and the cupboards are usually empty. If you would like to call me, you can do it on Saturday evening (my time) at (081) 868-2215. This is the number of Maria DeLuca, the woman living down the road. She also is a widow and we attend mass together every Sunday. I don't know what I would do without her. She is so good to me. Well, Jack, I look forward to having you and your lovely family. I am sure you will enjoy the beach down the hill. It is a bit crowded this time of the year, but it's convenient.

Until we meet here, God bless you all.

Jennifer

Becky flipped the letter on to the table, mumbling to herself. Valerie had just concluded an excited telephone conversation with Jack when she noticed her daughter's face.

"What's wrong?"

"I can't wait to see 'Little Becky," she mimicked. Laughter broke out between the two of them as they joyfully embraced. They were going to Italy!

DEPARTURE

(1)

"Ladies and gentlemen, this is your captain speaking."
The voice came crackling over the intercom of the elegant 400 passenger-capacity TWA 747 aircraft. "We will be flying at an altitude of thirty-five-thousand feet, with an outer air temperature of minus thirty degrees Fahrenheit. Along our route we shall be passing over a number of interesting sites, including the Pyrenees Mountain Range and the Island of Corsica. We anticipate clear skies throughout the flight and will point out these attractions as they come up. Our flying speed will be 620 miles per hour. Our scheduled time in the air is eight hours and forty-seven minutes, getting us to Rome's Leonardo Da Vinci International Airport at 10:00 a.m. Italian local time. On board we do have timetables for connecting TWA flights as well as those of other airlines. If we may be of assistance in any way, please do not hesitate to contact one of the crew. On behalf of myself, Captain McKinsey, and the crew of TWA Flight 840, I wish you a pleasant trip. Cabin attendants will now demonstrate the safety features of the aircraft."

The control cabin intercom clicked off as the recorded safety discussion began.

"The 747 Jumbo Aircraft are equipped with ten exits: five on the right side of the aircraft; and five on the left. In the unlikely event that cabin pressure is lost, oxygen masks will fall from the overhead compartments..."

The Jeffreys occupied seats D, E, and F, of row 57 in the plane's non-smoking section. Valerie nervously twisted a strand of hair around her index finger. Next to her, Becky's legs were trembling slightly. Neither of them had ever traveled by plane and their insides tingled with a mixture of fear and excitement. Even Jack, who appeared to be sleeping peacefully, had a spark of anticipation flickering through him.

The previous week had been hectic for all of them. Jack had spent most of the time taking care of last minute sales calls and getting airline tickets. They had cost more than he had expected. The TWA clerk had pointed out that it was the high season in Europe - meaning air fares were also at a peak. In addition, they had not booked in advance. Had they done this they might have saved thirty percent of the current purchase price.

Valerie had kept busy packing bags and cleaning the house. She still found time, however, to catch *General Hospital* and an occasional quiz show. In all the pre-vacation commotion her head was a maze of things to remember, though she knew very well that she would probably forget more than half of them. Even with all the preoccupation, a vivid memory of the dream had come back to her one afternoon. It had been nearly three months since the night she awoke in a sickening state of horror - the same night Jack had written the letter to Jenny. For days after, she had remained in bed, becoming sick every time her conscious mind brought the hideous face out of the dark dungeon of her brain in the form of a memory. Now, though, the recollection did not seem so terrifying. In fact, she found herself laughing at the thought of a nightmare making her sick for four days. But the pathetic, almost pleading look of the young girl who had turned into a putrid creature had haunted Valerie for the remainder of that afternoon.

Becky had kept herself busy trimming bushes, pulling weeds, and mowing the lawn as her father had requested. She hated the chores normally. But realizing that she would be well rewarded for her efforts made the tasks a little more enjoyable. In the girl's mind, Susan and Gary had accompanied her through the work. She was excited about the trip, but disappointed when she discovered that her friends would not be going along. As she worked, she continuously discussed her plans with the two imaginary companions, hoping to change their minds.

"Dad said Aunt Jenny lives in a castle...What? Of course she likes kids. She used to have a daughter, you know. She died in a fire or somethin'. I heard my mom talkin' about it the other day." Becky continued discussing the upcoming trip with the unseen Susan and Gary while she clipped the grass along the edge of the driveway.

Mrs. Davis, who lived in the brick fronted tri-level house two blocks away, was walking her white toy poodle down Lexington Drive, as she did every afternoon. Her head swayed from side to side in a pathetic gesture when she saw Becky chattering to herself. She was aware of the girl's mental problem, as was everyone in the neighborhood. It had become one of the best topics of gossip among the housewives' morning coffee circle.

From the large picture window, Valerie, too, had noticed her daughter. She had also seen Mrs. Davis' curious glances at Becky. It wasn't the first time a neighbor had done so and she hated them for it. They disgusted her. All of them. They looked upon her daughter as some kind of freak. And she was not. But they could never understand that. She would be happy to get away. Away from their glances. If Doctor Beaumont's theory was correct, Becky's problem would soon be over.

Jack stretched as the 747 bobbed in a sudden air pocket. He looked at his watch. One a.m. Pulling the thin silver stem he moved the hands ahead one hour so that it indicated the time in New York rather than Michigan. He remembered the stewardess taking away his tray after he'd pecked at the pre-fabricated food. But that was two hours ago. He must have been more exhausted than he had thought.

Becky was asleep and Valerie flipped through the pages of an *Ambassador* magazine, until her husband interrupted.

"Tired?"

"No. You?"

"A little." He stretched once again, covering his mouth to conceal a gaping yawn.

"How much longer do we have?" Valerie was becoming restless in the confinement of her window seat.

"Let's see." He pushed his shirt sleeve up slightly, revealing the black face of his Citizen Seven wristwatch.

"How long did they say the flight was?"

"I think it was nine hours."

"We left New York at eight. That was six hours ago. So there must be another three hours before we get to Rome."

Valerie had expected a similar answer, but hearing it made her restlessness worse. She let out a long sigh and tried to maneuver herself into a comfortable position.

"Put the seat back a little. Here, put this pillow behind your head and relax." Jack pulled the cushion that he had been using since the flight began from behind his own head and tucked it behind his wife's head.

"Feel better?"

"A little."

Jack settled deep into the seat and began thinking about his sister-in-law. Her letter had pleased him as much as it had the rest of the family, but at the same time it puzzled him. The way Jenny spoke of her neighbor - church every Sunday, and the God bless you sign off - it just wasn't like her. She had never been what one would call a churchgoer. Still, he realized that people change with time. Living in Italy as long as she had, it was probably inevitable that she should fall into the Roman Catholic faith, particularly after what she had gone through. It would be interesting to see what remained of the old Jenny and the differences with the new.

"Jack."

"Yeah, honey."

"How do you work these things?" From a little plastic bag, Valerie pulled out a pair of airline headphones.

"Where did you get those?"

"The stewardess brought them around when you were sleeping. Becky said she wanted to listen to music, then she dozed off."

"What'd they cost?"

"Nothing."

"Nothing! You mean we got something free?" He smiled.

Valerie had already placed the rubber tipped ends of the headphones into her ears, but there was no sound from the headset.

"I can't hear anything."

"You've got to turn this little dial." Jack reached over and flipped the dial. "Hear something now?"

The voice of Phil Collins came vibrantly bursting into Valerie's head as soon as Jack reached number three on the inflight entertainment selector.

"Turn it down!" she yelled, not thinking that she was the only one hearing the deafening sounds.

"Shhhhhh!" Jack turned the volume down, then pulled one of the plugs from his wife's ear.

"Better?"

"Much."

Valerie began playing with the various channels. Four, a song by Madonna. Five, classical. Six, seven, eight, nine, ten, eleven, twelve, and back to one. She finally settled for channel seven. It seemed to be all jazz. She enjoyed that. The music continued for about forty-five minutes before she realized that it was repeating itself. She listened to another fifteen minutes before the recorded program, once again, began its introduction.

"Jack, this keeps playing the same thing over and over."

"Change channels. Here," he handed her the *Ambassador* magazine, open at page sixty-four.

"The program listings are all right here. Just pick the one you want and turn the dial."

She glanced at the two-page listing.

How come she hadn't seen this when she looked through the magazine?

Halfway through the listing her eyes became heavy.

(2)

The *Ambassador* magazine slid to the floor as Valerie jumped with the intrusion of the stewardess' voice over the headphones.

"Ladies and gentlemen, please extinguish all cigarettes and fasten your seat belts at this time. We will be landing in Rome in ten minutes. Thank you... *Signori e signore, per piacere spegnete le sigarette ed allacciate le cinture. Atterreremo a Roma fra dieci minuti, grazie.*"

Rome? But Jack had said it would be another three hours. She had been listening to the Classical Hour with Carmen Dragon and must have fallen asleep. She removed the headphones and placed them into the pouch in front of her. Her left ear was sore from the jabbing rubber tip.

"Welcome to the world." It was Jack, smiling like a little boy who had just won a trip to Disney World.

"What are you all smiles about?"

"We're here."

"Rome? Already? What time is it anyway?"

"Three-thirty in the morning, our time."

"Three-thirty? I've been sleeping for two and a half hours?"

"You sure have."

"Hey mom," Becky broke in with a whispering laugh. "You even started to snore a couple times."

"Noooo. Jack, really?" Her husband chuckled softly.

"Why didn't you wake me up?"

"It wasn't so bad. And no one could hear you anyway."

Becky continued to giggle, until the plane suddenly began its descent. Reaching out, she grabbed her mother's hand. "Here we go!"

Once on the ground, Valerie and Becky found out that Rome airport was a far cry from New York's JFK, where they had made the connection from Detroit. They were transported from the airport to the International Terminal in what Jack called a cattle cart - a flatbed bus which carried thirty people at a time. Inside the terminal, passengers were hit with fumes of fresh paint. There were no workers, but signs of their presence were obvious. Scaffolding lined the walls and little beige dots of paint were splattered over the floor.

Valerie nudged her husband as they moved with the crowd towards the passport check.

"Look at the mess. I'd never pay painters to do this kind of work. They just leave everything and take off?"

Jack looked and shrugged.

"Probably *scioppero* today." A little man, obviously Italian, said next to Valerie. "I mean strike. Many, many strikes in *Italia* this day. Not like New York. You stay in *Italia* much time?"

"We're gonna be here a whole month," Becky was the first to respond. "We're gonna go to my Aunt's in Naples, then maybe Sicily too."

"Becky," Valerie interrupted.

The man smiled. A tooth was missing from the upper right side of his mouth.

"It's okay, she's a nice girl. My brother has a girl like her. He lives in New Jersey. I come from there now. You go to Napoli...*ahiii*! Always a problem...strike, protest, *camorra*. How you say? *Camorra* or *mafia*? *Camorra*, no?"

Before any of them had the chance to answer, they had reached passport control and were being herded around the booth by an eager pack of Italian-Americans.

"Where are the passports, Jack?"

"Didn't you put them in your purse in New York?" Valerie rambled through the Hudson's special value purse, but found no trace of the United States passports.

"Sure you don't have them?"

"I think you put 'em in your briefcase," Becky said. "Remember, you put 'em in there when you were reading the letter."

Jack looked at her questionably then handed the briefcase to the girl.

"Let's take a look. They've got to be here someplace."

Adrenaline was racing through both him and Valerie. What if they had lost the passports in New York? Oh God, thought Jack as he unsnapped the silver latches, what the hell will we do if they're not here?

A sigh of relief eased from his lips when, on the top of the brochures and airline tickets, his eyes discovered three tiny dark blue booklets with a gold eagle and the words *Passport, United States of America* imprinted on the covers.

"Told you they were there."

"And you wanted to give me the blame. Come on. We could have been through by now." Jack took the briefcase from Becky and the three of them headed into the crowd.

The lack of order - and single file lines - amazed Valerie. Another thing that seemed strange to her was the fact that there were four booths for passport control but only one was open, creating even more panic. Maybe there was also a police strike today? Just what she needed after ten-and-a-half hours in an airplane: crowds, lost passports, and striking police. She smiled, thinking of the little Italian man, who had now become lost in the crowd.

It took more than an hour to get through passport, baggage and custom checks and finally into the domestic air terminal of *Alitalia* where they turned their luggage in for the connecting flight. By now Valerie was getting her first taste of what Jack called culture shock. It seemed wherever she went in the terminal, armed *Carabinieri* were patrolling. She had read reports of the problems Italy had with terrorists. After the release of a few kidnapped high-ranking NATO officials, they had run a number of special reports on the problem on television. She had also read something about it in *Newsweek*. Like most of the world's problems, however, a flip of a switch made them go away. Here, though, it was obviously all around her. Real. And scary.

Jack would have preferred their trip to end in Rome, but there was still the flight to Naples and then a taxi to Jenny's home. She had offered to pick them up at the Capodichino Airport when Jack talked with her on the telephone. But the questions of late arrivals and her waiting in the tiny Naples terminal made it impractical. Besides, she had said that they had completed a highway connecting the airport and her area. What had she called it? The *tangenziale*. He had to remember that. Jack had learned from his last visit that unless you knew exactly where you were going, Neapolitan taxi drivers would profit by giving you a grand tour of the city before arriving at your desired destination, which might be only blocks from where you first began.

"Dad, when does the plane to Naples leave?"

"Another hour."

"Jack, why don't you change some money so we can get something to eat?"

"Good idea. I could use a good cup of coffee. You staying here?"

Valerie looked at him in a paranoid manner. "Are you kidding? All these guys running round here with guns and you want to leave me here? No way!"

"Come on Becky, let's go get some funny money," said Jack, heading for the *Cambio*.

The rate was 1650 lira to the dollar. Jack handed the smiling, handlebar-mustached man five twenty-dollar bills.

"Okay," said the man as he began counting colorful bills of Italian lire. "Onna-hunnded-a-sixty-fivva *mila* lire. Thanka you."

Valerie looked at the man behind the window. He had a pleasant, happy look - must like his job. Counting money all day would make her happy too. Especially if it was her own.

"Excuse me. Is there a place to buy a sandwich and coffee around here?"

"*Si, signora*. You see that sign there?" He pointed to the far left of the terminal building. "That one. You see?"

They thanked him and moved off in that direction.

"Look at this," Jack held a bill up so that the sunlight shone through it. "See that face? Look. No, here. See that? All their money is like this. There's a silver strip and a face in the paper. That's to make it difficult to counterfeit."

"Look at this one." Valerie had also gotten into the excitement of the Italian currency. "*Lire mila*. Who's this guy on the front, Jack?"

"I don't know."

"*G. Verdi*," he read. "Must be an Italian politician. Look, this one's got three little Greek goddesses in it. Here, Becky, look at this one in the sunlight. You see 'em?"

"Yeah."

"Do you guys want something to eat or not?" Jack's desire for a cup of coffee was growing. If he remembered correctly, you had to order a *cappuccino* in Italy if you wanted anything close to American coffee. The Italian coffee was coal black, thick, as strong as raw coffee beans, and it was served in what looked like doll house cups.

JENNIFER II

(1)

They had all become experts in Italian currency by the time they arrived in Naples and were headed down the *tangenziale* towards Baia. The airport bar in Rome had run out of milk, so Jack had settled for a café. Now, however, his stomach was paying for his bravery. He had been right about the taxi drivers - as they pulled out of the Capodicino Airport, the burly, Marlboro-smoking cabby had passed up the green *tangenziale* sign and was heading for a twenty-six mile route through downtown Naples. Jack had caught this though, and insisted they take the super highway. He had no idea where they were going once they left the main road, but periodically glanced up, said okay, then turned to wink at his wife and daughter who were taking in the scenery from the back seat of the tiny yellow Fiat 127. They had passed a small intersection and the sea had come into view on their left before the driver broke the silence enchantment of the new land.

"Ay, Joe, where go you?"

"Baia," Jack replied.

"Baia, *dove*?"

"What?"

"*Dove*, Joe. Where go? *Numero*, Joe, *numero*?"

"Jack, give him the address," said Valerie from the back seat.

"Here." Jack handed him the address while Becky and her mother laughed at the situation.

"*Via Roma? Via Roma?*" The cab driver repeated the words as if to trigger a memory, then turned the car right, stopping in front of a newsstand.

"*Senta, sa dova sta Via Roma?*"

Becky looked at her father, still laughing.

"What's so funny?"

"Nothing. What's he saying?"

"How should I know? I think he's asking directions."

The curly haired boy at the newsstand extended his hand towards the hill straight ahead and rattled off some slurry Neapolitan.

"*Aeiiiii...la' sopra*, Joe." The driver seemed to be disgusted at the fact that Jenny's house rested at the top of the hill, as he eagerly pointed out to Jack through a series of gestures.

David and Jennifer had purchased a large fourteenth century villa that had been built on the hill overlooking the Bay of Baia. It was a beautiful location, surrounded by an array of ancient ruins. From its south balcony one could see the sunken ruins of ancient Baiae as well as the golden dome of the antique cathedral in the fishing town of Pozzuoli. To the west lie the Bay of Bacoli. And slightly north, though not visible, were the remains of what was once the Italian capital of Greek civilization, the acropolis of Cumae. The seclusion and historic surroundings were the determining factors that made David purchase the villa more than ten years ago. After the fire, the house had been completely redecorated following Jenny's decision to remain on the hill. It was a splendid place, but the dirt road that led to it was, as the cab driver put it, *male* for automobiles.

No sooner had the taxi pulled up than a thin, semi-gray haired lady, clad in a knee-length black dress, came rushing down the marble steps of the huge castle-like villa.

"Jack!" It was Jenny. Older and simpler than he remembered, but nevertheless, it was her. As she drew closer, he noticed her skin was still firm and dark. She reminded him of the retirees that spent their lives in the Florida sun.

"Jenny!" He jumped from the front seat of the car and met her with an embrace at the white gate.

"You look great, Jack. Just great." Becky and Valerie had now climbed out of the pill-box Fiat and began walking towards the reunion, when Jennifer looked up.

"Valerie!" she said, breaking the lock around Jack's shoulders. "I'm so happy to have you here. You haven't changed one bit. Still as young as ever."

Valerie could not say the same for Jenny. It was obvious in her dress and manner that she had changed. "How have you been, Jenny?"

"Oh, just great. Just great. It gets a little lonely up here by myself, but when it does I go into town or visit Mrs. DeLuca. She lives just across the street there." She stretched out her arm and pointed to a three-story apartment building about a hundred yards down the bumpy dirt road.

"And this is Becky," said Jack, pulling his daughter forward.

"*Mio Dio*, Jack. I expected a baby. This is a full grown young woman."

Becky liked the comment. And she liked her aunt. She was different. Friendly. Had a nice smile. And when she extended her hand, Becky eagerly met it with her own.

"How do you do, *signorina*?"

The girl blushed at the formality of the situation.

"Becky. Answer your aunt," urged Valerie.

"Well, thank you."

"How was the trip?"

"Not bad," said Jack. "We slept most of the way."

"But I'm still tired," Becky said, smiling at the older woman.

"Are you hungry?"

"I don't know about them, but I sure am," replied the girl.

"Becky!" Valerie interrupted, giving her daughter a glance as if to say remember your manners.

The girl looked towards the ground, but was saved by her aunt's interruption.

"Sure you are, sweetheart. Look, there are no manners around here. If you want something, just holler at old Aunt Jenny. Okay?"

"Okay," replied Becky.

"Come on now, let's go inside and get you all settled. I've got everything prepared. Maybe you'd like something too, hey Jack? Food I mean? Valerie?"

"Okay, Jenny. But first, let's get settled. We've got plenty of time."

"*Signora!*" The taxi driver had pulled the luggage from the tiny trunk, untied Jack's plaid suitcase from the car top and placed them in a neat row beside the gate.

"Oh, the taxi." Jack reached into his pocket and pulled out his black imitation leather wallet. "Jenny could you ask him how much it is?"

"Sure. *Quant'e*?"

"*Quanto? Undici mila e cinquecento, signore!*"

"He wants eleven *mile* five hundred, but don't you pay it. *Ti do nove mila lire, niente di piu!*"

"*Ma signora...*" The driver began waving his arms, frantically protesting. Jack stood there with the Italian money in his hand, not knowing what to say or do.

"Here, pay him what he wants and let him go."

"NO! He's a thief. Just like all of them. *Nove e basta*! Here," she pulled a ten-thousand lire note from the bundle. "Give him this. *Ecco, addesso vattene!*" With that, she grabbed a tiny suitcase, and walked up the stairs. About half way, she turned to the others.

"Come on! Grab the bags and leave him there. He'll go away."

Following her instructions, Jack and Valerie picked up the remaining luggage and headed for the house. She had been right. No sooner had they reached the wooden front door than the taxi drove off, the driver calling out obscenities to Jennifer.

"Thieves. They'll try to get every penny they can then turn around and say you tried to rob them. Some nerve, huh?"

Inside, the villa was luxurious. They left the bags at the entrance as Jennifer took great delight in giving them a grand tour of the rich structure. The floors, except those of the bedrooms and bathrooms, were a glistening polished white marble. In the center of the huge living room, a crystal chandelier shone like a star in the heavens. To the right was the kitchen, completely lined with patterned ceramic tiles and green, hanging plants. Next came a large bedroom that had been prepared for Becky. On the opposite side of the house was a hall leading to the formal dining room, the downstairs bath, Jennifer's bedroom and a wood-paneled library. In the corner of the receiving room an elegant staircase led to the upstairs landing, which supported a fine polished, wood banister. The steps were made from the same smooth white marble as the rest of the house.

As they headed for the steps, Becky noticed the door that had been incorporated into the underside of the stairs. Aunt Jenny had made a point of showing them every inch of the first floor, but had not even mentioned where that door led.

"Aunt Jenny."

"Yes, sweetheart?"

"Where does that door go to?"

"Oh, I'd forgotten about that. Probably because I never had the cellar redecorated."

"A cellar? What's down there?" Becky fantasized the thought of trap doors and secret passages in such an ancient place.

"I use it to store vegetables, wine and bottled tomato sauce. That's about all it's good for. You won't have any reason to go down there. Now let me show you the upstairs."

Directly ahead was the enormous master bedroom, decorated in a blue and white wallpaper, where Jack and Valerie would be.

"The bathroom is down there to the right. There's plenty of cupboard space, clean towels and things like that. If you want to take a bath or shower, it is best if you do it in the early morning or late in the evening. Living on the top of a hill, I sometimes run out of water in the summer. This year, it's not so bad. I'm without water only a couple of hours on Saturday and Sunday."

Turning left, Jennifer led them down the hall, past a large sitting room with antique velvet-clad furniture, and to a metal trimmed glass door at the end of the corridor. Jennifer turned the key that rested in the lock and pushed. Direct sunlight beamed through the opening, momentarily blinding them. The door led to fifty square meters of balcony, bordered with white wrought iron railings and covered in one corner by a woven bamboo canopy. It overlooked the seaside, extending slightly over the mountain cliff. Under the protective canopy were randomly scattered a small table, two chairs and a body length sun seat.

"This is where I take the sun," said Jennifer. "You can get direct sun all day and don't have to worry about crowds or tracking sand into the house. The only thing it doesn't have is the sea. But I'm not much of a swimmer anyway. The beach is down there," she tipped her head upwards as if to point the direction with her chin, "if you prefer it. But, usually, there are so many people that you can't move."

Jack walked to the far edge of the balcony. It was quite a drop to the winding waterfront road below.

"A long fall," he said, as the others joined him.

The last rays of sun came streaming like pastel-colored floodlights over the mountain to the west. The few altostratus clouds that lingered in the sky took on an appearance of red fireballs with the reflection of the setting sun.

The four of them stood motionless admiring the moment, until Jack turned to his wife.

"Look at this. Isn't it beautiful?"

"That's one of the reasons I'd never leave this house," said Jennifer. "On a clear day you can even see Capri and Ischia. And when they have sailboat races on the bay it almost looks like a picture." Her words drifted off into the warm, mellow breeze and Valerie noted a glimmer of cherished memories in Jennifer's tone. It was a sad sound. A sound of loneliness. And Valerie could feel herself becoming sorry for the woman.

She was alone. Alone in this enormous, beautiful house for all these years.

"Well!" Jennifer broke the stillness. "Enough of this. You'll have plenty of time to see the view. Now that you know where the balcony is, feel free to use it whenever you like. For that matter, the entire house is at your disposition. But it's best..." the words were cut short, as if she were reconsidering what she was about to say.

"Best if what, Aunt Jenny?"

"Nothing, Becky, nothing... Come on, let's go fix something to eat and decide what we'll do tomorrow."

Single file they reentered the house as they had come, through the small metal door.

Jennifer had to be more careful. She had almost slipped, but hadn't. That was the important thing. But she definitely had to be more careful about what she said.

TOURIST I

W hile Jennifer prepared dinner, the visitors unpacked, showered and became settled in their rooms. Their first taste of Italian food had been what Jennifer called typical. They had begun with spaghetti and clams. Then came heaped plates of mixed squid, shrimp and fish, followed by pastries and ice cream. Jack had been delighted when Jennifer offered to make coffee, but lost his enthusiasm when she pulled out the tiny Italian pot. Not wanting to disappoint his host, he had forced a tiny cup of the black syrup down his throat.

It had been dark for more than an hour when Valerie and Jennifer completed washing the dishes. Prior to retiring for the evening they had sat in the kitchen discussing possible activities for the following day. Becky wanted to go to the beach. Valerie had hoped to see Pompeii and the National Museum of Archeology. Jack preferred to spend the day relaxing on the huge balcony while taking in Italy's warm late August sun. He had been warned that Mediterranean summers can often come to an abrupt rainy end during September and the one thing he wanted most, besides a good rest, was a golden tan. After hearing Jennifer's descriptions of the many ruins of the area, however, his old college daydream began to flicker within him and his thoughts of lazy days in the sun faded.

"We can see Pompeii next week when the summer crowd thins down," said Jennifer. "Believe me, you'll enjoy it much more then. Right now it will be like a zoo with the tourists. Come the first of September, though, you'll hardly see ten or twenty people. If you want to see ruins, Valerie, we can go to Cuma. It's only a couple of miles. I'm sure Mrs. DeLuca would drive us there."

"Isn't that a Greek site?" interrupted Jack with awakening enthusiasm.

"The oldest one in Italy, so they say. According to historians and archaeologists, Cumae was settled by the Greeks in the eighth century B.C., two hundred years before Pompeii, even before Paestum. Supposedly, ships would pull into the port of Cumae and soldiers would march through huge tunnels which led from the acropolis, under the mountains and come out somewhere in this area of Baia. You can still go through the first section of the tunnels and come out onto the Via Vecchia Cuma. Then it keeps going on the other side of the road, but the government closed that section off after World War II. If not, you could go all the way through to Lago Avernus, I guess. A volcano in the 1300s destroyed whatever there was of the rest of the tunnel."

"Imagine that, Val. A tunnel running all the way across this peninsula. Just think of how long it must have taken. Centuries? It's not like they had jack hammers and steam shovels."

"Oh, that's just one. There are thousands of tunnels all over Italy. But especially around here. I remember a few years ago along the Via Domitiana - that's the road you took when you got off the *tangenziale* highway - the entire street caved in from heavy rain. It's no exaggeration to say that the hole was the size of this house. Some people said a couple of cars went in, but I don't know if I'd believe that. Anyway, after the rain finally stopped, they found out that the hole was actually part of a huge tunnel. Another time, in Naples - or was it Rome? - well, I can't recall, but they found an underground cave that had been used as a headquarters for car thieves. They would drive the cars in, paint them, change tags, and store them right there. That's how big some of these underground caves are."

"What about the one at Cuma?" asked Jack. "Why won't they let people go through it?"

"They say the Germans used it as an ammunition depot during the war and that much of the explosives are still there."

"Wow, kinda-like a spooky story," said Becky.

Valerie, who sat across from Jennifer, turned to her husband. "Well, what do you think? Cuma? Pompeii? The museum? Or just sit around and rest up?"

"Or to the beach!" added Becky from the opposite end of the heavy pine-stained table.

Jack looked at his watch. Ten minutes after five. He had forgotten to change it at the airport.

"What time is it, Jenny?"

"Eleven-ten," she said, looking up at the tiny German cuckoo clock that hung next to the refrigerator.

Valerie looked at Becky then Jack. "So late?"

"You forgot we're six hours ahead here," he laughed. "Tell you what, why don't we decide in the morning, okay?"

Valerie nodded and yawned.

"Come on, Becky." Jack stood up. "We gotta rest up if we're gonna play tourist."

"But I'm not tired anymore."

"Let's go," said Valerie, taking her daughter by the hand to pull her from the chair.

All of them exited the kitchen and headed for their assigned rooms. All, that is, with the exception of Jennifer. She had stopped downstairs outside the bedroom door where Becky was to sleep.

On the upstairs landing, Jack and Valerie turned to their sister-in-law.

"Not going to bed?" asked Jack.

"No, not yet. I still have a couple of things to do first. I'm something of a night owl around here. So don't be alarmed if you hear someone shuffling about, it's only me."

"Okay, goodnight."

"Goodnight, sweet dreams."

"Night, Jenny," said Valerie, closing the door behind them.

The woman looked through the door at Becky.

"Everything okay?" The girl was just slipping the blue and white nightgown over her head.

"Yes, thank you."

"Want me to close the door?"

"No, that's okay. Would you shut the light off though?"

"Of course I will, honey." Jennifer smiled as her niece climbed under the fresh, cool sheets.

Becky turned and smiled at her aunt. "'Night, Aunt Jenny."

"Goodnight, sweetheart."

The light switch clicked and instantly the room became deathly black. Becky heard her aunt return to the kitchen. The woman's face was still vivid in the girl's mind. Smiling tenderly. But there was something about her eyes that was scary. A chilling tremor raced through the girl's spine. Trembling, she pulled the sheet taunt over her shoulders, around her throat, and closed her eyes.

(2)

It was 2:15 when Jack woke with a sensation that he was still in the 747 aircraft. His eyes blinked frantically as he shook his head into the reality of where he was. Still, even with the sudden awareness of being in his sister-in-law's home, there was something wrong. He fumbled through the dark for the night stand light switch.

Click! A radiant glow filled the room.

Jack froze, momentarily. In a single instant his mind raced like an overloaded computer for a solution to what was taking place. Overhead he could see the tiny chandelier swaying back and forth. The night stand was trembling as was everything else in the room, including the bed. Something fell to the floor with a crashing sound. Jack whirled his head, pinching the nerve in his neck. Pain, like hot needles, shot from his skull and along his neck. It was a couple of seconds before he could move his head. And when he did, it was painful.

"*Ahhhhh*!"

By now Valerie had begun to stir from her dreaming state. "Jack? What's the matter?" Her words were slurred and filled with unawareness.

The pain had finally subsided. Now fully awake and in control of his senses, Jack once again surveyed the room. The furniture movements had stopped. And, if not for the continuous swaying of the chandelier, he might have passed the entire episode off as a dream. In front of the dresser, a bottle of Valerie's Noxzema had shattered over the floor.

An earthquake! Jack sprang from the bed, into his slippers and robe. Valerie was snoring again, completely unaware of what had taken place.

No need to wake her, Jack thought. As long as it doesn't start again, she'll be better off sleeping.

He eased the door open and was halfway down the steps when Jennifer flipped on the kitchen light. Jack jumped in surprise, nearly slipping off the steps.

"Everything okay?" she whispered.

"Yeah, I think so." he said, placing his hand over his chest as he tried to catch his breath.

"What's going on? An earthquake?"

"*Shhhh...* come on into the kitchen. Becky didn't wake up. Valerie?"

"Asleep too."

"Better that way. Keep from getting scared for nothing."

He held his questions until they were settled at the kitchen table.

"What happened?"

"Bradyism."

"Bradyism?"

"Happens quite often around here. But not quite as strong tonight."

"What is it anyway?"

"Just a minute, let me get something."

Jennifer shuffled out of the kitchen, and returned with a tiny magazine rolled up in her hand. She flipped through the pages, then suddenly stopped, obviously finding what she was after.

"Here," she handed the booklet to Jack. "Read it while I make some coffee. It'll explain everything."

"No coffee for me, thanks."

"Would you prefer tea?"

"If you're going to have some too. But don't make it just for me."

Jennifer began rummaging through the cupboards while Jack looked at the magazine. It reminded him of a *TV Guide*. He slipped his finger between the pages that Jennifer had indicated so as not to lose the place while he looked at the cover: *R & R In The MED, March '97*. There were three photographs on the cover.

Jack didn't recognize the four men in the first picture. They were obviously a rock group. He did recognize singer Alison Krauss in the photo on the lower right hand side. The third photo was a scenic shot of someplace... *Invitation to Ireland*, he read along the lower edge of the cover. On page 55 he saw, *Ghost Town of Pozzuoli*. This was the article Jennifer had wanted him to read.

"Don't tell me. Ghosts were moving the house."

"Just read the article."

A modern day Pompeii that reveals the eerie remains of what once was. The sub-title sounded interesting, but what does a modern day Pompeii have to do with the earthquake... or whatever it was?

Jack began to read the article, though he would have much rather preferred that Jennifer explain the tremors.

"After living in the Naples area for several years, I thought..."

The article had a dry introduction, but he continued. Then, in the second paragraph, he came across what looked like the answer.

"The Phlegrean Fields area, particularly Pozzuoli, has always been known for its natural phenomenon of bradyism (rising and lowering of the land). Over the centuries, some parts of this district have sunk as much as 65 meters..."

Now intrigued, he raced through the short feature, discovering that the area had sunk drastically since the time of the Roman Empire due to the land-moving: bradyism. The main part of the article talked about the area in Pozzuoli that had to be evacuated in 1967 because the earthquake-like movements became so bad.

"You mean this happens all the time?" Jack asked, putting the magazine on the table.

"No, not all the time. About once every two or three years."

"Why don't you move?"

"What for? I've got everything right here. You expect me to pack up because of a little shake? Oh sure, it gets a little scary sometimes. Especially when you're alone. But it doesn't happen that often and you learn to expect it every now and then. Did you read about the Roman times?"

"Yeah, it said this even happened back then."

"Only worse. You know, divers have found a sunken city right out here in the bay. They say it's the original Baiae. According to theories, it sank into the sea because of this bradyism. Remind me tomorrow. If it's a nice day we'll be able to see it from the balcony. You know, you can't really tell what it is, but you can make out black areas in the water."

By the time they finished their discussion, two cups of tea each, and returned to their rooms, assured that the house would not move for another two to three years, it was 3:20 a.m.

Jack kicked the pieces of broken glass into a pile and climbed into bed next to his wife. He didn't think he'd be able to sleep, but fifteen minutes later he was in a land of unconscious dreams.

Before going to bed Jennifer had checked each of the downstairs rooms for damage. A few books had fallen from the top shelf of the library, but other than that everything was in its place.

The house was stuffy. Hot. Humid. Typical, in Naples, during the summer. Jennifer went through the house randomly opening the long door-like windows which led to the outside. A gust of cool sea air whisked through the halls as she braced the windows so that they remained open about five inches. She would have to close them first thing in the morning or flies would start coming in. But now, the slight breeze was just what the house needed.

THE CREATURE

(1)

The trembling earth roused the creature that lay huddled in the corner of the damp musty root cellar. Its eyes rolled uncontrollably, trying to focus. The sound of its respiration filled the tiny room, echoing against the hard packed floor, finally being absorbed by the dirt walls. The creature leaped to its feet. Realization finally registered in its tiny, feeble mind. Something was wrong! The security of quiet and darkness had suddenly been broken. Its eyes widened, showing the piercing pupil surrounded by a glow of white. A dog-like growl seeped through its rotting yellow teeth. Its hindquarters now pushed hard against the muddy wall as a prickly sensation rose along the back of its neck. It was a creature of the dark! It loved the dark! It was protected by the dark! But now! Now! The darkness was closing in. The room was alive! Instantly it leaped. The little shelter was breathing. It was as if the creature were trapped inside a human lung that instinctively opened and closed. Escape! It must escape! It crawled across the quivering cellar to the heavy wooden door which had begun to rot along the bottom. Its long, dirt-filled claws began ripping at the splintered wood. Splinters tore into its flesh, causing dark, cherry-red blood to flow down its gnarled hand. But the creature did not stop. Fear had taken control of its senses and the animal's instincts triggered escape in its brain.

Dust flew from the monster's hair as it continued its fruitless attempts for freedom. Clumps of dirt began to fall from the wall at the far end of the room. Slowly, at first. Then faster and harder the earth began to fall in from the once-solid wall. The creature turned, trembling, wet, frightened. The refuge it had cherished for so long was now becoming a tomb! Suddenly, as rapidly as it had begun, the movement ceased. Silence, once again, filled the dark room. There was a feeling of suffocation. Long snake-like hissing sounds protruded the creature's dry, cracked lips as it sucked in air to fill its heaving lungs. It was alive. Safe.

Nearly an hour passed before the creature moved, then another thirty minutes before it eventually slid its way to the crumbled wall. But, there was something wrong! The room was no longer as it had been. The creature climbed over the fallen soil. Where once the protective wall stood, there was now a large hole... and a distinct but dim glow of light. The creature slithered through the freshly made opening. On the other side was a room. It was not like the room the creature had left. It was smooth, cool and shaped like a dome. The walls and floor were not covered by soil, but by something unknown to the monstrous being. And the light! Yes! There was light! From the far end of the mysterious room, moonlight radiated through an arched opening - the opening that led to paradise. The creature knew this. It had come. The time had come to return to paradise. It had done penitence for the sin committed. Now, its reward was near.

Slowly, haltingly, the creature crawled the three steps that lead to the opening. Tall briar bushes covered the exit, concealing it from the outside. These, however, did not stop the creature. It had smelled the winds of paradise and now pulled at the thick weed stalks as it slithered through. The tiny thorns poked the creature's hanging flesh, ripping it in places. But it did not care. Lying on the side of the mountain, it did not care about the trickling droplets of blood. It was free.

It had come to love the darkness, like a child with a security blanket. And now, its eyes flickering at the moon, it had found peaceful darkness even here, in paradise. It could roam at will under cover of night. But it would have to return to the tomb. That much it had remembered… in paradise, there was also light.

And with light came man. Man, who created evil. Man, who created hate. Man, who would destroy the creature, had it the chance. It had been Man who put the creature into the earth. But now it was free, smarter, wiser. It would continue to be a thing of the dark. When light came, it would return to its refuge. Man would never find it.

But now there was much to do, to explore, to learn. The creature's subconscious had stored many memories waiting for this moment. Now, as it began to scale the mountainside using its hands and toenails like climbing spikes, these memories began to flash through its mind. They were jumbled, foggy. But one thing was clear: the hideous creature was only paces from the mountain top and the villa that rested upon it. And it was there that it would find the answers.

UNSEEN FRIENDS II

(1)

Becky was perspiring. The tips of her hair were wet and the thin cotton nightgown damp. The sheet that had covered her lay on the floor as she had kicked it off in her sleep. There was an evil presence hovering in the humid atmosphere. A smell. An air of something evil, but tangible.

Though asleep, Becky clairvoyantly sensed someone or something in the room, causing her to turn restlessly. She had been sleeping surprisingly well considering the time change, the strange bed, and the room temperature. She had not even moved during the sudden earth movements, remaining curled up like an unborn child in a mother's womb. Now, however, the dream-like sensation of being watched was bringing her back to the conscious world.

Becky had had these feelings before. They were always the same. Susan or Gary would be standing beside the bed trying to wake her. Then they would want to talk about something or other. They never touched her, but could wake her up mentally, just like they were doing now. And, though she could not stop them, she had grown used to it.

In her half-awake state, the girl kept her eyes closed, thinking that she was in her own room. She waited for her unseen friends to begin talking. She knew one of them was there. She could feel it. There was heavy respiration, almost a panting, coming from one corner of the room. It must be Gary. Susan would never overexert herself to a point that would cause her to breathe so desperately.

Becky waited. Silence. She wanted to go back to sleep, but knew it would be no use trying until Gary left. But why didn't she say anything? She lay there, her eyes still closed, a few more seconds. Then, arching her back in a long stretch, she broke the stillness.

"What d'you want, Gary?"

No reply. Becky, began to notice the smell that had been but faintly registered while she slept.

"Gary, what's that smell?"

She waited for an answer. But there was only dead silence, broken by the continuous breathing from the darkened shadows.

"Look, Gary," her words carried a tone of returning sleep. "I know it's you. If you're not going to talk, leave me alone. I'm tired."

She was on the verge of sleep when the sounds of shuffling filtered into her ears. Why would Gary be walking like that? And why didn't she answer her? She had never done that before.

Thump!

Becky's eyes opened. She was awake now, completely alert. She was not in her own bed. She was at Aunt Jenny's. And Gary was not there. Both he and Susan had remained in Michigan. Her hands grasped frantically for the fallen sheet. Quickly she pulled it up around her neck for protection. It would hide her from whoever was watching her.

Thump!

The girl's head turned to the right. Though her movement was rapid, she felt as if she were engulfed in an aura of slow motion. The bedroom door was wide open, its brass handle bumping against the wall. She no longer felt the presence, nor heard the breathing. But the distinct odor lingered. An odor of mold and decaying flesh. An odor that made her sick.

There was only one light switch in the room, next to the door. Becky felt an urge to run towards it. But, at the same time, she was rooted to the spot, under the safety of the sheet. She was no longer a child that could call her mother whenever something frightened her in the dark. But there had been something there in the room with her. She was sure of that. But who? Or, she trembled at the visions in her imagination - *what?*

Throwing off her security, Becky raced for the brass light switch.

Click! Radiant beams of salvation flashed upon the room from the five-bulb chandelier.

Nothing! Whoever it had been was gone, leaving the door wide open in their escape. A gust of fresh air rolled through the open library window at the other end of the house, racing down the hall to cross the large living room and rush past Becky. It felt good, clean, refreshing.

In the light, the incident seemed more like a dream. Even the horrid smell was no longer evident. It must have been a dream, she thought, looking around the elegant room. Nothing. At least nothing that didn't belong there.

She turned her wrist and glanced at the silver Timex. It was 4:33 a.m. It would be light soon. Slowly she closed the door, and turned the skeleton key until the lock clicked into place. She would leave the light on, but preferred the adults not find out.

With the door locked and the light on, Becky returned to the bed and the security of the sheet. Though she was sure it had all been a dream, in the back of her mind she could not shake the reality of the situation and how it resembled the wake-up tricks that her friends Gary and Susan often played.

It took her a long time to doze off. And even then, her sleep was restless. Every fifteen or twenty minutes she would wake startled and trembling. By the time the sun did finally come up, Becky felt and looked as if she had been awake the entire night.

(2)

Following Jennifer's suggestion, Jack decided not to mention the strange bradyism movements of the previous night. He had gotten up early to clean up the mess of glass and cream on the floor and was half finished when his wife looked up from the bed.

"What are you *doing?*"

Jack jumped as if he had been caught stealing something. "*Ahhh*...I...I knocked this off the dresser. Sorry, honey. Maybe Jenny knows a place we can pick up another one."

"Don't worry 'bout it, I brought two." She slid back under the sheet and closed her eyes. No need to rush. This was a vacation.

(3)

Becky and Valerie had finished a toast-and-egg breakfast by the time Jack came downstairs freshly shaven, showered, and wearing a new navy blue cotton shirt and a pair of white tennis shorts.

"What would you like for breakfast, Jack?" Jennifer asked.

"Anything is fine. No coffee, though. It's a little too strong for me."

"Tea?"

"Okay."

"Eggs and toast?"

"Sounds fine." He pulled a chair away from the table, causing it to squeak across the marble floor.

"Well, what did we decide?"

Valerie looked at Becky and Jack. "Nothing. Becky wants to go down to the beach. I don't really care. And I don't know what you want to do."

She seemed depressed.

"Becky, could you get a couple of eggs for your aunt?" Jennifer interrupted. "Two or three, Jack?"

"Two will be okay, Jen." He was staring at his wife. Something was bothering her, he could tell.

Becky stood up and began walking towards the refrigerator as Jack leaned towards Valerie.

"What's wrong?" he asked in a whisper.

Valerie put her index finger across her lips as if to hush him up. Jack's look went from concerned to puzzled. It was not like her to keep secrets.

"Dad, I want to go to the beach."

"Becky, let your father decide what he wants to do. If he wants to take you to the beach, fine. If not, you can go some other time. Jack..."

"I wanna go to the beach. Don't you, Dad?"

"What?" Jack had been gazing at the cuckoo clock, as the smell of frying eggs filtered through the kitchen. Only half of the conversation had registered. He was thinking of Valerie. What was she hiding? Was something wrong with her? Was she sick? Maybe she really was angry about the broken skin cream jar? Maybe he should have told her the truth? Perhaps Jenny had said something to her after all?

"You want to take me to the beach, right?"

"Jack, what would *you* like to do today?" Valerie's tone still contained an air of depression.

"I'd really like to lay out on the balcony. I didn't sleep too well last night."

"That's what I was thinking about too," said Valerie, looking up at her sister-in-law. "Do you need some help, Jenny?"

"No, no. Stay where you are. Here you go." She slid a plate in front of Jack. "Toast will be ready in a minute. And here's your tea. Valerie, would you like another cup?"

"No, thanks. I still haven't finished this one yet."

"Oh, Dad! I don't want to sit up there all day. I want to go to the beach. What kind of a vacation is it if you can't go swimming'?"

Jack looked at his wife. Neither felt like leaving the house, at least not today. At the same time, however, the trip had been planned primarily for their daughter.

"Look," Jennifer said, taking a gulp of the coal-black coffee. "Why don't you two spend the day on the balcony and I'll take Becky to the beach. It's only down the hill and I've got to walk to *Arco Felice* to do some shopping anyway. I can take her down, get her settled, do my shopping, and pick her up on the way back."

Valerie was the first to protest.

"No, one of us can take her. There is no need to bother yourself."

"What bother?"

"C'mon, Mom!"

"It'll really help me more than it will be a bother if I have her to help me carry some things up the hill. What do you say, Jack?"

He looked at Valerie. The feeling that he had become a buffer zone between the two forces came over him as he swallowed a mouthful of egg.

"Seems all right with me."

"It's settled then. Becky, you help your aunt clean up and a little later we'll take off. No need to get going before eleven. The sun really isn't up until then. Okay?"

"Okay," said the girl.

"Oh, Jack. I forgot your toast!"

"Don't worry about it."

"I'm sorry."

"This is fine, really." He sipped the hot tea. He had never had it with lemon before. Jenny must have put it in out of habit. It wasn't bad. He would enjoy a couple hours sleep on the balcony after last night.

(4)

Upstairs, behind the closed door of their bedroom, Jack finally confronted his wife.

"What's wrong with you?"

"I'm worried about Becky."

"Why? What's the matter?"

"She said someone was in her room last night. Or at least she thought so."

"She was probably dreaming."

"When has she ever dreamed about someone in her room?"

"Lots of times. She's always saying her friends wake her up in the night, remember?"

"That's what worries me. They're not dreams. It's her imagination." There was a moment of silence between the two. Jack realized what his wife was trying to say.

"I don't know, Jack," she said in an almost crying state. "We spent all this money because Doctor Beaumont said it would help, and the first night here she sees someone in her room."

"Maybe Jenny looked in on her."

"No. She said that whoever it was didn't say anything."

"Strange."

"I know. At least these imaginary friends talk at home... she even slept with the light on."

Jack pulled the suntan lotion out of his wife's beauty case and flipped a brown Gary cloth towel around the back of his neck.

"Did Becky seem upset when she told you?"

"A little."

"More than you?" He smiled, leaned down and kissed Valerie, who was sitting on the bed. "Tell you what. Why don't you forget about it? Sounds to me like she was just dreaming. Put your bathing suit on, I'll be waiting for you on the balcony." He kissed her again, long and hard. "If you're lucky, I may even give you a Coppertone massage."

She smiled. "Guess you're right. Maybe I am getting upset for nothing."

"Come on, honey, forget about it." Jack walked towards the door, his mind at ease now that he knew what had been bothering his wife. "See you - in the sun - in five minutes."

"Okay. Want your book?" she asked, raising the half-finished paperback western that he had begun reading on the plane to Naples.

"Might as well. If I can't sleep it will save me coming back for it."

"Be there as soon as I get my suit on."

"Okay, but hurry. The master masseuse may be asleep soon."

"Get out of here."

(5)

Jack had been on the balcony fifteen minutes. The sun was hot and felt good on his bare, white skin. He'd have to be careful not to stay in the direct rays too long. He was just beginning to turn onto his back when the door opened. The sun was directly overhead, blinding him every time he opened his eyes.

"That you, Val?"

"No, it's us!" Becky's voice rang out.

"Still here?"

"Yeah, Becky and I decided that you might like some refreshments a little later. And, since we won't be here, we've brought everything up here."

Jack sat up to see his daughter and sister-in-law setting an array of fresh fruits, soft drinks, iced tea and snack foods on the tiny white table.

It was then that Valerie came through the open doorway.

"What's going on?"

"Aunt Jenny and I brought you guys some things in case you get hungry."

"You didn't have to go to all that trouble, Jenny."

"No trouble. After all, no need for the two of you to be running downstairs every time you want something. Now you've got everything right here when you want it. Just help yourselves. Anything else I can get for you?"

"No, you've already done too much."

"That's right," said Jack. "The two of you go do whatever you have to do now. Becky, mind your Aunt Jenny."

"Jenny, you sure she's no trouble? We could take her."

"Look, you two just leave us alone. You shouldn't have any reason to go downstairs. So enjoy the sun and we'll see you in a few hours."

Valerie picked up a freshly washed apple, bit it, and tossed it to her husband. Becky and her aunt had walked across the tile flooring and were just about to close the glass door when Valerie stopped them.

"Jenny! Have you decided what we're having for dinner?"

"I thought spaghetti, then maybe chicken. Why?"

"Maybe I could get it started while you're shopping. That way you won't have to rush." There was a touch of guilt building up in her after seeing the pains Jennifer had taken to make their stay easier. She wanted to repay the favor.

"Noooo. I've got everything laid out and it won't take me a minute to prepare. You just stay here and enjoy the sun, you hear me!" With that, she closed the door. Valerie had noticed a slight tone of superiority in Jennifer's voice. Almost as if she had been giving an order. Jack also noted it, but decided to let it pass.

"See?" he asked.

"See what?"

"You were so worried about Becky. There's nothing wrong. Just give her some time."

Valerie smiled, looking down over her husband. His eyes were closed, and in between his words, he chewed tiny bites of apple.

CRACK! She slapped his exposed stomach.

"Where is my massage?" They both laughed as he pulled her on top of him in the lounge chair.

THE CELLAR

(1)

It was three o'clock. Jack had fallen asleep two hours ago. Becky and Jennifer had still not returned and Valerie had become bored. She waited another fifteen minutes on the huge balcony, then went into the house to slip into a cotton jumpsuit and sandals.

She admired the beauty of the house while walking down the stairs towards the kitchen. She'd love to have a place like this back home. The ceilings must have been at least twelve feet high and fine cut marble seemed to be everywhere. Jenny had told her that it was abundant in Italy, making it a relatively cheap building material. Wood, on the other hand, she had explained, was extremely expensive due to the lack of forests. Strange, Valerie thought, as she entered the kitchen, in the States it was just the opposite - at least in Michigan, where everything seemed to be made of wood.

Like Jennifer had said, everything to prepare dinner was laid out on the table - uncooked *La Molisana* spaghetti that had been precisely measured out for four people, salt, thawed chicken legs, parsley, olive oil, and a bowl of fresh fruit.

"Cuckoo!" The tiny German cuckoo bird popped through the miniature wooden door of his house advising the world that it was 3:30, then slipped quickly back into its mechanical security cage.

Jennifer and Becky would be home soon. She might as well begin to get things ready; it would take a while for the chicken to cook. She opened the top of the Italian *Becci* oven. It was a gas model, easy enough to understand. Jenny must have matches around the kitchen somewhere. Valerie finally located a box of wooden *fiammifeeri familiari* in the tiny drawer next to the sink. She lit the front burner and placed a pan of water over the open flame.

By the time Jack stuck his head through the doorway, startling his wife, she had chicken frying, water bubbling, and was going through every cupboard in the kitchen looking for tomato sauce.

"What *are* you doing?" He laughed seeing his wife sitting on the floor.

"Looking for the tomato sauce," she said, almost hitting her head on the open cabinet door, as she turned. "I thought you were asleep."

"I was." He smiled slyly, then walked across the room to Valerie. "But I couldn't stay away from you." He gave her a quick, unromantic kiss on the top of her head.

"Well, Romeo. Why don't you help your Juliet find the Ragu?"

"I thought Jenny said not to worry about getting dinner ready."

"She did, but I'd say the same thing if people came to our house."

"If you say so."

She stood up, stretching her cramped legs. "I give up. I've looked every place."

"Jenny said she keeps tomato sauce downstairs, want me to go get some?"

"Tell you what. You stay here and watch the chicken. I'll go get the sauce."

"Yes, Mistress, your wish is my command," he laughed and slapped her on the buttock. "But hurry up. I don't want to be blamed if this burns."

"You will be," shouted Valerie from the living room.

(2)

She reached for the knob and opened the door which led to a small stairway. Enough light seeped through the opening for her to see the way. Suddenly, about three-quarters of the way down, there was an eerie feeling that she had been here before. The narrow stairway. The dark brown door at the bottom of the steps. The silver key which opened it was not in the lock. It was in Jennifer's red apron that Valerie had slipped on when she began cooking. She reached into the pocket. Yes, it was there. But, how had she known? And why was everything so familiar?

She slipped the key into its place. The door to the cellar eased open under the pressure of her hand. Valerie could feel the humidity engulf her. There was a smell of mildew in the air. She had a reason for being here. Though, despite her efforts, she could not remember what that reason was. She stood silent for a moment. Slid one foot forward. There were two steps ahead, she knew it. But how could she know? And the light switch to the left. There would not be much light even if she did switch it on. There was only one thirty-watt bulb hanging at the far end of the basement. Her head was full of knowledge of the place. Knowledge she should not have. But did. How could she know? She had never been here before. Or had she?

What did the scientists call it? Déjà vu. That was it. This was the first time that she could recall it ever happening to her. She seemed to contract through the dark chambers of her mind. The answer must lie somewhere inside her.

"Tomatoes," she whispered. It was all she could recall. It was enough, though. Enough to bring her back to reality. It was tomatoes, or rather tomato sauce, that she was here for.

The sudden realization had broken the aura of mystery. Yet, in the depths of her subconscious, she had not forgotten.

She flipped on the light. It was barely bright enough to outline objects in the room. Quickly she moved to the western wall and found shelves lined with green-glassed, one liter bottles. She recognized the red and white *Ferrarelle* labels as that of the Italian mineral water that Jennifer always had on the dinner table. But that was not what the bottles held. Jennifer, like many women in Italy, had reused them for bottling tomato sauce.

Valerie reached out and gripped two of the dusty bottles by their slender necks. Then froze. Perspiration broke out on her brow. She began to shake. She had done this before! And she now remembered when. Like a shooting star that looks small in the distance, then grows as it rushes towards the earth, the tiny embryo of the memory that she was unable to bring back previously, had suddenly expanded, filling her mind. Her head. Her body! The room! It was all there! Just as it had been before...before...in...in her *DREAM*!

With the trip and all, Valerie had had many things to occupy her thoughts. So, the dream, which had made her feel so uneasy and sick in the United States, had been pushed aside. Now, however, it was vivid, alive. And, this time, real!

Her mind reeled in rebellion. She had gone from the eerie sensations of déjà vu to the horrifying reality of premonition.

"*Nooooo...!*" The word came out stressed and stuttered.

The moldy odor that had been so distinct now seemed mild compared to the mounting smell of human excrement. Though impulses relayed to her legs and feet to escape, they did not respond. She was helpless. Fear had taken sole command of her body.

The smell was overbearing, yet Valerie refused to acknowledge it. Whimpering sounds like that of a young puppy emanated from her. It's impossible, she thought. It can't be there. It can't be. But it was possible. The ultimate fear which she now remembered so well.

Her head began to turn to the right. It was not by her own will she moved, but rather the powers of terror that gripped her. She knew what she was about to see. *THE EYES*! They were there! Like two burning lights in the darkness! The eyes were there, embedded in the horrible and distorted face that supported them! The hideous gurgling sounds came mumbling from the creature's gaping mouth.

"*NOOOOOOO!*" Valerie's body became limp, clammy, cold, and moist. Hot urine was running down her legs. Her eyes could no longer see. Sound was blocked from her ears. She was unconscious to the living world as her body collapsed to the cold dirt floor.

(3)

When Valerie came to she was in bed. Jack was sitting next to her. He had heard his wife's scream and rushed out of the kitchen, through the living room and stumbled down the stairs which led to the cellar. He could barely see in the basement, but made out the figure of Valerie sprawled on the cool packed dirt floor. Quickly he swooped her up and began to carry her out. Suddenly he stopped. There was a strange, dank odor in the room. He looked around, but saw no one or anything. At the far end of the basement was a rotting wooden door swaying slightly. Once again, he surveyed the space, nothing other than the usual cellar stored items. He then rushed his wife to their upstairs bedroom.

Jennifer had returned five minutes later with Becky. In the kitchen, she had found the chicken burning and water boiling. The girl had gone directly upstairs in excitement, to tell her parents her experiences at the beach.

"Aunt Jenny! Come upstairs! Mamma's sick!"

Valerie's sense of awareness was just coming back when her daughter and sister-in-law entered the room. Her mind was boggled, fogged, as if a circuit had blown. The only thing she recalled was that something was in the cellar. She began to cry and pulled Jack down to embrace her.

"What happened?" Jennifer exclaimed.

"I don't know, she..."

"It was there," sobbed Valerie. "In the basement. It was there."

"*Shh*... calm down, honey. It's all over."

"No, Jack. It's down there."

"What's down there? Honey, there isn't anything in the basement. I was there, baby."

"The basement!" The tone of Jennifer's voice sent a chill down Jack's spine. He turned and looked into what appeared to be the face of death. She had become a pale white. Her left hand gripped the railing of the large brass bed, squeezing it until the veins bulged a deep purple from under the skin. The left hand trembled in a spasmodic rhythm.

"What were you doing in the basement?" She did not wait for an answer. "Jack, you shouldn't have let her go down there! The light's terrible. She probably fell or something!"

"No, Jenny," Valerie's voice was filled with fatigue. "I saw something down there. It was horrible."

"Valerie! Now stop it! I was down there too."

"Did you see anything?" questioned Jennifer.

"No, no, nothing."

"What did you see, Valerie?" Jennifer was after more. She had to know every detail.

"I went downstairs for the sauce. When I found it, there was that... that thing!" Tears began to flow down her cheeks once again. Becky moved next to the bed and took her mother's hand.

"It's okay, Momma."

"Oh, Becky."

"Well, I'm going to have a look! You and Becky stay here with Valerie."

Jennifer rushed out of the room and was in the musty cellar within seconds. She knew exactly where to go. The root cellar. That tiny little room that had been dug out of the ground as an extension to the basement. If there was something there, it would be in the root cellar.

Her heart pounded. Breath rushed in and out through her mouth. She stood motionless for a moment. Then, as a shot of blood-flowing adrenaline sent fire-like sensations through the body, sensations of fear.

The root cellar was open! With hands that shook like a junkie without a fix, Jennifer opened the door. Nothing! The room was empty. There were gouge marks around the lock of the door. On the floor was a long, thin steel pipe. Whatever terrorized Valerie so had used the instrument to break through the lock and enter the home.

A light shone at the back of the root cellar - a light that should not exist. Slowly, Jennifer stumbled through the darkness in a crouched position. There was an opening! And from it she could see another room, larger and covered with glittering tiles. On the far side of the room was a sequence of steps that led to an opening on the side of the mountain just below her home. A direct access to the cellar.

Perspiration flowed from every part of her body. She began to run back through the root cellar, catching her foot on the clumps of loose dirt. Her head hit hard against the ground. Dirt sifted through her teeth as blood began to seep from the front of her gums. Like an escaping snake she crawled out of the dark pit and slammed the door behind her. She stood, pushing her back against the door as if to keep the demons of hell from being released upon the world. Her breasts heaved up and down. She was dirty, sweaty. Blood ran from the corners of her mouth. Mud had stuck to the left side of her hair. But that didn't matter. None of it mattered. There was only one thing on her mind: the root cellar was empty.

She wheeled around and looked up at the nail to the right of the door. The key was still there. She eased her hand forward. It was trembling worse than before. Snatching the silver key, she slipped it into the lock. If she could lift the heavy door slightly, it still might work. Her white face became red as she strained to push the door up. It was almost there. A little more. Animal-like grunts came spewing from her lips.

Every ounce of energy her body contained was going into her frantic struggle.

CLICK! She had succeeded. It was locked. What had entered the basement was now trapped outside.

Jennifer's eyes rolled from side to side. A smile of insanity crossed her face. She began to laugh, spitting blood and dirt with each babbling chuckle.

Suddenly she was silent. Her mouth closed. A serious expression covered her face. It was as if a switch had been pulled in her mind. Nothing was in the root cellar.

JENNIFER III

(1)

For two days Valerie had remained in bed trying to convince herself that it had all been a dream. Finally, on Thursday, Jack talked her into a trip to one of the local sites. Getting out of the house would do them all good, he had told her. The atmosphere had changed since the incident in the cellar. Valerie was constantly depressed. Becky was disappointed because no one would accompany her to the beach. And Jack was preoccupied with his wife's health. But the big change, he had noticed, was in Jennifer.

She had come up from the cellar and gone directly into her room the afternoon of Valerie's vision, as she called it. In fact, Jack thought she was still down there when he called her two hours later. She came out of her downstairs bedroom, clothes changed and hair neatly brushed, but he had noticed a nervousness about her. During the course of the evening she had assured him that she found nothing out of the ordinary in the basement, but she continued to give off an aura of uneasiness. He had merely passed it off as a normal reaction to all the excitement that had taken place.

The next day, however, Jennifer appeared more tense than ever. She became startled at the slightest noise. Then she would disappear, not to be seen for hours. Her features were white, sunken, and the sockets of her eyes dark as if she had not slept the entire night.

On Wednesday evening Jack had found a colorful tourist guide to the Grotto della Sibilla in Jennifer's library. The site was not far from the villa; about a half mile walk. It would be a great place to go, he had thought, and it would also be a change for Valerie. She needed to get away. To forget whatever it was that her imagination had conjured up in the cellar.

Jennifer was in the kitchen. She looked worse than the previous day. He had asked her to come with them to the cave, but she had come up with some off-the-wall excuse to stay at the villa.

Becky was excited about the excursion. "Anything to get out of the house," she had said.

Valerie, however, was undecided. She sat twirling her hair, mouthing something about not feeling up to it. But Jack had lived with her long enough to know that she was merely dodging reality, like a child who is frightened to leave the security of her bed in the dark. Her excuses continued, including the possibilities of bad weather.

"Okay," he finally told her, not wanting to show his disappointment at her actions. "We'll see in the morning."

He woke at two-fifteen that morning. His bladder needed relieving. Quietly, he slid out of bed, not wanting to wake Valerie. She needed her sleep. He wondered what dreams were flowing through the canals of her mind as he looked down at the dark, tangled hair that covered her face.

The marble floor felt cool on his bare feet. It was a good sensation, completely the opposite of the hot, humid atmosphere of the bedroom. He slid the door open and stepped onto the landing. The bathroom was just down the hall; there was no need to turn on the light. He took two steps, then stopped. He cocked his ear and froze, like a field dog on point.

The distinct sounds of someone locking a door came from downstairs. Then a voice. It mumbled, and Jack could not make out everything. But, from the tone, he could tell it was his sister-in-law.

"Again... again... *again*... why? Why did it? I don't have any choice! No choice! No choice. No! *Hah*! It knows that. It knew it. Yes, yes it did. I've got to find it... right... right... First, we have to find it... then... then... we know," a smile came over the woman's face,"....yes...*we know*." The words came out fast, jumpy, ranging from soft whispers to squeals of insane laughter.

Jack eased toward the edge of the banister. She had been in the cellar. Something was wrong. The way she talked to herself. There was definitely something about Jennifer that was mysterious. Quickly he jumped back, not wanting to be discovered as the woman made her way through the living room and down the hall to her own bedroom.

He remained on the upstairs landing for a few minutes trying to put the puzzle together. It made no sense. Something was happening in the house. He could feel it. It had begun the day Valerie went into the cellar. But what could it be? Whatever it was, Jennifer was part of it.

He leaned forward. The coast was clear. Quickly he returned to the bedroom. The need to go to the bathroom had been forgotten.

(2)

Jack was up at five. Following the strange events that had taken place that night, he had slept restlessly. Finally, he gave up, dressed and went downstairs. In his head, he still sought the key that would open the door to this mystery that surrounded Jennifer's behavior. There had to be something. And that something was probably in the cellar.

Downstairs, Jack passed through the long hall, heading for the library, until he got to his sister-in-law's room. The door was open, but there was no one inside. He continued on his way to the library. She was not there either.

During the next five minutes he searched every downstairs and upstairs room, including the balcony. Jennifer was not in the villa. Unless... he raced down the stairs to the door which led to the basement. It was locked. Where could she be at five in the morning? This was not the first time she had vanished in the past few days. Until the previous night, though, Jack had never really thought of seeking out her whereabouts.

The basement! This would be the perfect time to find out what was so mysterious about the cellar, without Jennifer finding out. But he'd need the key.

He made his way through the house towards the kitchen, stopping to look in on Becky. She was sleeping. He closed his daughter's bedroom door and went into the kitchen. He knew where to look for the key and went directly to the red apron. His hand shook with excitement as he felt inside the deep pocket. It was not there. Jennifer had moved it.

He drew a chair from under the table and sat in silence, looking around the room. Where could she have put it? Probably in her room, tucked away in one of the drawers. Maybe she was carrying it with her? Or maybe... Jack stood up. He hurried from the room and rushed down the hall to the library. There was an old, wooden roll-top desk in one corner. He had seen Jennifer sitting there more than once over the past few days. It was worth a look anyway.

He pushed at the thin wooden cover, expecting resistance. There was none. It was unlocked and rolled easily into its open position. Jack began going through the drawers systematically. Paper, buttons, a few coins, screws, nails, letters, but no key. In the center drawer were three photographs. He recognized his brother, looking handsome in his Navy uniform, and an early photo of David and Jenny holding a baby. But the third picture, obviously a school photo, was of someone he had never met. It was a girl, perhaps in her early teens. She was pretty in a simple way, with blond hair and blue-green eyes. But there was a red birthmark on the left side of her face that kept her from being what Jack would call beautiful.

He was fairly positive, but his thoughts were confirmed when he flipped the photo over and read ANGELICA. It was his dead niece.

"Jack!" Jennifer's voice struck him like a bolt of hot lightning, sending warm flashes through him.

"Do you need something?"

"What? Ah...no, no." His thought processes were working at a speed far greater than that of light and he immediately had an excuse for his presence in the library.

"I wanted to write a letter, but couldn't find any paper." To give his alibi even greater support, Jack reversed the questioning as he slid the pictures back into the drawer and closed the desk.

"Where were you? I looked all over before I started searching around on my own, but you weren't here."

"I couldn't sleep, so I got up early and went for a walk." Her tone was different. She had switched from being the accuser to being the defendant and, now, preferred to drop the discussion altogether.

"Anyone else up yet?"

"No."

"What would you like for breakfast?"

TOURISTS II

(1)

Thursday morning, Valerie felt better than she had since their arrival in Italy. She had managed to push the face in the cellar to the back of her mind, where, hopefully, it would be recalled only at her will. Jack must have already awoken and gone downstairs, she thought, easing to the side of the bed, dangling her feet over the edge.

Tiny rays of streaming sunlight shone through the gaps in the wooden shutters. It was a beautiful day and she wanted to get out, to leave the villa for a while. As far as that went, she wouldn't mind leaving it forever. The place was beautiful, but it scared her. There had been at least two people killed in the villa... David and Angelica. And, as old as it was, who knows how many others might have died here. In this very room. She had read about places becoming haunted by the spirits of past owners who had been violently killed, like that place in Amityville a few years back. But, even with her keen interest in the occult, she hadn't believed any of it. That is, until what had happened in the basement.

Valerie had gotten up and begun dressing when Jack came into the room.

"Morning," he said, flopping full length on the bed.

"Morning." Valerie pulled a pair of cream-colored Bermudas over her revealing lace panties.

"You look good today," Jack smiled, watching her dress. She returned his grin and fastened the gold zipper.

"How you feeling?"

"Not bad."

"Feel like going out?"

"That's what I'm getting dressed for."

"I'd better get Becky up then." Jack stretched, then stood and walked over to his wife. His arms slipped around her slender waist. Slowly his head bent down to hers. Before their lips could meet, however, Valerie turned her head away.

"No. I haven't brushed my teeth yet." She puckered up and met his semi-parted lips for a brief second.

"Now go get your daughter up while I fix myself. And find out if Jennifer's going with us. If not, make sure you know where we're going."

"Yes, Ma'am," he said, backing out the door and onto the landing.

(2)

Taking advantage of Valerie's renewed interest in seeing some of the local sites, Jack decided to make a day of it. Following Jennifer's advice, they would first visit the Grotto della Sibilla, pick up a couple of sandwiches on the way back and spend the remainder of the day at the beach. Jennifer had preferred to stay in the villa. She had said that she wasn't feeling too well and Jack had not insisted, noticing that she looked a bit pale.

Jack was not sure of the entire story behind the mythological grotto they were about to see, but he knew that it was supposed to be the entrance to hell that had been used by Aeneas in

Virgil's *Aeneid.* Jennifer had drawn directions to the site. It was within walking distance of the villa, around Lago di Avernus.

Jack, Valerie, and Becky had walked down the hill, along Via Miliscola, past Lago di Lucrino, until they came to a news-stand and a road leading off to their left. Two bright yellow signs pointed toward the road. One read: Lago d'Averno; the lower one: Grotto della Sibilla. The road had been paved at one time, but was now full of chuck-holes, some as large as a washtub. It was a good half-mile to the entrance of the cave, but the tall pine trees that lined the road and the smell of wild flowers made the walk enjoyable.

Once at the Grotto della Sibilla, they noticed an old man standing beside the lake. He looked up and smiled, then began to move towards them.

"Americano?" He continued to smile.

"Yes," Jack replied. "We're American."

"I think so. I am Enzo. Enzo Rossi. You would like tour of grotto?"

"Yes, but aren't there people who are supposed to give guided tours? I mean, official guides?"

"*Si, si.* I. I am custodian. Come on, we start at lake, then go to cave."

The man had a pleasant look about him. Jack estimated his age to be around sixty-seven or sixty-eight. Yet his face seemed full of life. Covering his tanned forehead was a crop of thick, powder white hair. Unlike the skin of most elderly folks, his hands and cheeks were tight and smooth. He was one of those interesting people that instantly seem to be an old friend even though you have never met.

"What see you today is no what was during Roman time." His English was poor, but understandable. He also realized this.

"If you don't understand, please tell me. In ancient world, Lago di Avernus was like Solfatara of Pozzuoli. It was volcano with mud bubbling up and fumes rising into sky. Because fumes has poison sulfur inside, birds flying over would die and fall into inferno, according to Virgil. This is where *Avernus* comes from. In Latin, means - no birds. When Vesuvio erupt in 79 A.D., all volcanic action stops here and crater fills with water. In Roman times, Agrippa built canal connecting Lago di Avernus with the sea and the fleet would anchor here. In 1538, Monte Nuova erupt overnight and fill lake part way -cutting it off from sea. Also, eruption cut off tunnel that leads to the underworld. Before, the cave of Sibilla was much long and deep. Charles III of Bourbon," he raised his hand and extended three fingers to illustrate his discussion, "was interest to excavate the ancient cave which Virgil make famous. In 1700s he make tunnel to intersect the original one." He gestured with his hands to better put his point across. "But it began in the middle, so today, is only half as long as in ancient world. Do you understand?" Glancing quickly about, he continued the lecture. "Now we go into the grotto. Inside is dark, so stay near me."

Jack had heard of many strange things that occur in Italy, the liquefying blood of San Gennaro, people nearly killing themselves at the annual *Madonna del' Arco* festival, and the unquestionable shroud of Turin - but as he ventured through the dark cave led by Rossi's voice, which came out in a vapor because of the cold temperature within the earth's depths, and a flickering candle-like carbon burning lamp, it was as if mythology were coming true before his eyes.

"Wow! Isn't this something?" he said, looking over at Valerie and Becky, who had put their arms around each other in the haunting shaft.

Signor Rossi went on, "Many people confused here with the Sibyl of ancient Cumae. But, must remember! There were many oracles in Greek time. Cumae Sibyl was most powerful, most near gods and with the control that could not die. The Sibyl of this grotto was like a priestess. She listened to man, talked through echoing cave and gave advice. I like here. It is my job for much time. At Cuma, is no guide to Sibyl's cave. People are scared. Cuma Sibyl had much power, like I say *prima*...before, before. And still many feel her presence there."

By the time they reached the legendary River Styx, about 200 meters into the black cave and to the right, Signor Rossi had them also wondering whether they should see the Cumae site or not. His fear of the Cumaen Sibyl was evident and Jack was fascinated by the idea that people in the area would continue to worry over a being that had died 2000 years earlier.

"According to Virgil, Charon carried the dead across this River Styx on his boat. I am modern day Charon. When I was young, I carried people to the other side on my back, like my father and grandfather before me. Soon, my son will take over as fourth generation."

From the supposed River Styx, they were escorted deeper into the cave and down to a second level where, according to the guide, the not-so-powerful priestess would speak with the dead and fulfill her role as the local oracle.

"Is that it?" Becky whispered to her mother.

"No idea, honey."

The old man's English was poor but he had caught the conversation. "No. Still more."

What followed was a number of interesting as well as mysterious underground sites to be seen by the light of the flickering lamp. And, by the time it was over, the three of them felt an extreme satisfaction with both the fascinating cave and the guide. They had gotten a one hour tour of Lago di Avernus and the Grotto della Sibilla. In exchange, Signor Rossi asked ten *mila* lire. Jack was happy to pay the small fee and felt they had gotten a bargain, and they had.

(3)

There were not many people at the beach: half a dozen teenagers, an older couple, Jack, Valerie, and Becky. It had a private access only to those paying a monthly fee. Jennifer had taken care of everything for them when she and Becky had come the first time. Jack had protested her paying for them to use the beach, until she explained that the owner was an old friend and had given them access, umbrella, and a *cabina*, where they could change, free of charge. All they were to do was go into the fenced area, mention her name and have a good time.

Jack could not forget the fascinating cave. The guide had said there was a similar one in the ruins of Cuma that was historically more important than the one they had seen this morning. His mind wandered, imagining the history that must have occurred in this area...the Greeks, the Romans, the Barbarians. It fascinated him. He, too, might have been discovering unknown treasures and archeological sites in exotic lands, had he not met Valerie. And now his hopes of becoming a famed explorer of ancient civilizations had long since passed. Still, that did not keep him from becoming excited over the local sites and the history that went with them.

Valerie and Becky had been splashing in the cool, calm saltwater for five minutes when three scuba divers came from the bay carrying yellow net game bags and pulling a red and white divers' flag mounted on an inner tube. Jack, in his daydreaming state, had fallen asleep under the shade of the large, two-colored beach umbrella.

"Dad!" Becky came running through the hot sand. Jack sucked in a deep breath of air, rubbed his eyes, and looked up at his daughter.

"What is it, Becky?"

"Some guys just came out of the water with a bunch of junk and Momma said to come and get you."

"What guys?"

"Scuba divers. They speak American, too."

"Scuba divers?" he repeated, trying to figure out why his wife would want him to look at some starfish or seashells a scuba diver might find. Then he remembered what Jennifer had told him the night of the tremor... oh, what was it called? Bradyism. That was it. Yeah, there was an ancient city in the bay.

Quickly he got to his feet. Scuba divers. Maybe they had discovered something. Scientists perhaps? Becky said they spoke English. The thoughts continued as he walked towards the shore where a small group of Italians had gathered around the three, clad in black wet suits.

"What's up?" he asked, moving in next to Valerie.

"These guys found all kinds of things. They're Americans."

"How do you know?"

"Listen to them."

Jack did listen. The more he heard, the more excited he became. And when the divers began to expose oil lamps, bits of pottery and tiny chips of what appeared to be tiles, he could no longer resist questioning them.

"You fellas American?"

All three looked up, somewhat surprised to hear his perfect English.

"Yeah," said the youngest of the group.

"I'm Jack Jeffrey. I'm on vacation here with my family. You guys live here?"

The tall, thin diver with an almost white beard and matching hair stood up and extended his hand to Jack.

"Bill Thompson, pleasure. That's Jerry Smith," the younger diver nodded. "And Mike Freeman."

"Pleasure."

"We're in the military, stationed at AFSOUTH. That's the NATO base here."

"Not all of us," said Mike Freeman, the oldest of the group.

"Mike's a history teacher," said Thompson.

"I knew there was a base here. My brother was stationed there. But that was quite a while ago. You found all this stuff out there?" Jack nodded towards the open bay.

"Yeah, there's a sunken city out there. Fifteen, sixteen years ago - when was it Jer, '80 or '81, that they found the statue down here?"

"1980, I think," came the reply.

"Anyway, every once in a while something important comes up. But I think most of it has been pretty well cleaned. They've done about six or seven official underwater archeological digs. All that's left now are bits and pieces. We were lucky today. Got an oil lamp."

"What are these?" Jack asked, pointing at the shiny stones that looked like they had been coated with glaze.

"Tesserae. You know, pieces that were used for mosaics."

"Really? Are there any mosaics still down there?"

"A couple. *National Geographic* had an underwater camera crew here a few months back doing some special on underwater cities of the Mediterranean or something. They found about three mosaics. None really anything more than Roman floors. I mean nothing like you'd find in Pompeii."

"How old is the city?"

"I read an article in one of the base magazines, *Overseas Life*, I think it was. It said the city used to be old Baiae. Supposedly it was like the Riviera is today. You know, rich Romans, orgies, parties. Musta been some place, huh?"

"Even Nero had a place here," said one of the others. "Historians say that he tried to kill his mother here."

Jack's curiosity had completely overcome him by now and their words drew him deeper and deeper into the archeological world that he could never enter.

"Where can I get a copy of this magazine? What did you call it?"

"*Overseas Life*. I don't know where you'd get a copy now, unless you write to the magazine. The article came out a couple of years ago. It almost caused some trouble for us, telling the world that we were robbing the city of treasures that weren't even there."

"What do you mean? It talked about you guys? I'm sure there must be all kinds of divers that find things down there."

"Sure there are. What I meant was that the article badmouthed the dive club. See, we're all members of the Sub Aqua Dive Club. We've got a couple of urns and some pottery, an old anchor, and who the hell knows what else gathering dust around the club house. It's been there for years. But this jerk writer comes in, sees all of it, and tells everyone we got it from the city."

"What are you going to do with this stuff?"

Mike Freeman pulled the quarter wet suit over his head, unstrapped the Scuba Pro knife from his leg, and began placing the recovered objects back into the net carrying bags.

"We'll take them to the Minister of Antiquities," said Thompson. "They'll probably laugh and give us a permit to keep it all."

"Really? They let you keep this stuff?"

"Shit, this is nothing. The area is full of ancient treasures. These things are *nothing* compared to some of the things people find. Like that statue they brought up from here. It's in that castle over there if you wanted to see it." Thompson extended his arm and pointed to a large castle on the hilltop across the bay. "That's the Baiae Castle. There's a whole collection of statues up there."

"Anyway," Mike Freeman interrupted. "To answer your original question: the sunken city, which was the original Greco-Roman Baiae - that's spelled with an '*e*', not like it's spelled today - dates back to before Christ. Are you familiar with Livy?"

"The ancient writer?" asked David.

"Yes. Well, he wrote that this, what is now the sunken city, was the playground of the Romans, full of villas, pavilions, baths. It's really an interesting place. I'm working..."

"Yes, professor. Tell us about your projects," Jerry joked, holding the end of his Scuba regulator up like a microphone to his partner's mouth, as if he was a reporter.

The four of them laughed. The crowd had broken and gone back to their lounge chairs and umbrellas.

"What I was about to say is that I received a grant to do some studies here three years ago. Then, one thing led to another, the grant ran out, and I began teaching history at the University of La Verne. It's an off-campus program for the military.

"And your research?" Jack was intrigued with the opportunity to talk with a scholar of Roman antiquity.

"Still ongoing. Who knows, maybe someday I'll get enough information to write a book. There was an article in one of the newspapers a couple weeks ago about the theory that there was once the richest tomb in existence around this very area."

"Really? Now that's something!" exclaimed Jack.

"It would really be something if I could put enough evidence together to locate it. I know it's around here somewhere. From the old manuscripts I've studied both here and in Rome, it was supposed to be on one of the hills around here. The damn problem is that volcanic activities have created new hills and eliminated probably half of the ones that existed during the early Greek times."

"You mean the tomb goes back that far?"

"So they say."

The three divers had collected their gear and were about ready to head for their car. Jack felt more excitement now than he had in years. These guys were doing what he had always desired. To them, it was nothing to discover ancient pottery. To him, it was a life's dream.

"Is there any way I could get a copy of that newspaper article?"

"I've got a couple of copies. If you'd like, I'll give you one," said Mike Freeman.

"I'd be really grateful."

"I've got a class at the NATO base tomorrow at noon. But I'll probably be there around ten or so to pick up my mail. If you could meet me there I'll bring the article in."

"That'd be great."

"You know how to get there?"

"No, I'll take a cab."

"Don't waste your money," said one of the others. "The local train stops right here next to the beach every fifteen minutes. Costs 900 lire. Catch it heading towards town, get off at the Bagnoli station and you're there. The base is about fifty yards away."

"Great," Jack said, helping them carry the heavy tanks across the beach to the highway.

"Once you get to the front gate, you'll have to call me and I'll come down. With all the terrorist problems, they don't take any chances letting people just walk in."

"I can understand that," replied Jack. "I don't imagine it would take much to have another kidnapping on your hands."

"Right. Anyway, when you get there call extension four-five-five-nine. That's La Verne. I'll be there until twelve."

"Okay, see you then. Take care - and nice meeting you."

"Same here. See you tomorrow."

Jack's hand made a salute like a wave as the blue Fiat 850 drove off. It had been an interesting encounter, one that he had greatly enjoyed. He looked forward to the following day's encounter and the possibility to discover more about the area's historical past.

JACK

(1)

That evening at the dinner table, Jack spoke of nothing but sunken cities, ancient ruins, and tombs. His archeology ambition had become so stimulated by the meeting with the divers that he did not even notice Jennifer's continued nervousness nor sense the strange odor that had begun to fill the villa.

"So, I'm supposed to meet the guy tomorrow morning at the NATO base."

"Oh," said Valerie in an uninterested manner.

"Yeah, I thought you and Becky could go to the beach. We'll walk down the hill together. I'll leave you two at the beach, catch the train, and meet you when I come back."

"Sounds good to me," said Becky.

"How do you know the train goes to the NATO base?"

"The guys told me. It does, doesn't it Jenny?"

"Yes, yes of course. You get off at Bagnoli."

"See. It'll work out perfectly."

Valerie could not keep from noticing how much older Jenny looked this evening, and the air of tension around her. Perhaps it would have been better if they had stayed in a hotel.

"Why don't you come with us tomorrow, Jenny?"

"Me? No, I've got things to do in town."

"Then you can go down with us," said Jack.

"Come on, Aunt Jenny."

"I guess that would work out. You know, I've really been thinking about going to Naples. There's something I need to pick up there." She stopped and gazed into the corner of the room as if trying to make a mental connection. "Yes, I guess that would work out. Since everyone will be out of the house tomorrow, there's no need for me to stick around. I can take the train with you," she said looking at Jack. "I'll show you where to get off and continue into Naples. Yes, that sounds like a good idea."

Valerie was happy that her plan had worked. Jennifer needed to get out of the villa, to be around people. Jack had told her that he heard Jenny talking to herself the other night. It must be terrible to lose your family and spend the rest of your life living alone.

(2)

Valerie was in front of the dresser mirror rubbing Revlon Intimate perfumed moisturizer onto her face. Jack was lying in bed rereading the article on the ghost town of Pozzuoli that Jennifer had shown him nearly a week earlier.

"Did you notice Jenny this evening?"

There was no reply from her husband. He was engrossed in the story in the tiny magazine.

"Jack!"

"Yeah, honey?"

"You didn't even hear me, did you?"

"Every word, honey. Did I hear what Jenny said this evening, right?"

"Wrong. I asked, did you notice Jenny this evening?"

"In what sense?"

"You know! How nervous she was."

"Yeah, I guess so. She's kind of strange sometimes. You know, I wonder if she's all there."

"Jack!"

"Well, I do. Like the other night. Honey, she was really out of it. Talking to herself, laughing. I mean, it reminded me of that movie where Jack Nicholson goes crazy. Remember? What was the name of that film? You know, the one where he's a writer and takes a job for the winter at some lodge."

"*The Shining.*"

"Yeah, that's it. That's just what she sounded like."

There was a break in the conversation. Valerie was putting drops in her eyes and Jack had returned to the magazine.

"There was a funny smell downstairs, wasn't there?"

"A little. Maybe a dead animal outside."

"Maybe," she said, climbing into bed next to Jack.

"Aren't you gonna shut off the light?" he asked.

"You're reading, aren't you?"

"I was. I'm finished now."

"Well then, get up and shut off the light."

Jack smiled, he felt great, and Valerie had a sexy smell about her that aroused him. Like a leopard he sprang from the bed, his bare feet slapped on the floor as he scampered across the room, clicked the light switch and returned to the bed. Under the thin sheet once again, he cuddled up with his wife. Instinctively, their moist lips found each other in the dark. Jack's right hand felt warm on Valerie's leg as it eased upwards, under the light blue lace nightgown.

THE TOMB

(1)

The ten-fifteen Cumana train pulled into the Bagnoli station ten minutes late. Jack had gotten up early, prepared eggs, toast, and tea for everyone. He now sat receiving specific instructions from Jennifer on how to get to the NATO base from the station.

"Once you get outside the station, turn right, go down the little alley for about twenty meters. You'll see a tiny overpass on your right. Make sure you look before going through - it's just large enough for a small Fiat. After you've gone through that you can see the base in front of you."

"Okay," Jack said as a group of teenagers began to push him towards the opening doors. "See you tonight."

Jenny did not reply, just nodded her head and attempted to smile.

The train was hot, musty, and wall-to-wall people. The moment the train's electronic glass door opened Jack leapt to the paved sidewalk and a rush of fresh air.

Bagnoli station was layered in dust and pornographic graffiti. As Jack walked out the front entrance into the hot September sun, a whistle sounded and the train pulled away, heading towards the Mergilina station. Jennifer would remain aboard until Piazza Garibaldi, in the center of downtown Naples.

The cobblestone streets were filled with the fragrance of vegetables, fruit, and fish. On one corner, just before the tiny arch that Jack had to go through, was a display of fresh lobster, octopus, tuna, and a number of other sea creatures caught by local fishermen in the deep Mediterranean waters. In one plastic tub were what Jack figured to be at least fifteen live eels, frolicking in rhythmic circles. In a smaller and shallower tub were dozens of live clams, many of which had come out of their protective shells and were shooting streams of water, like miniature squirt guns.

Jack had become intrigued by the array of edible marine life, but it quickly faded when a burly, hairy-armed fisherman walked over to him and began to talk. Though Jack could not understand a word, it was obvious the man expected him to buy something. Smiling, Jack continued along his route.

The front gate of the NATO base was a mass of *Carabinieri*. Two stood in the center guard house, directing entering traffic and checking IDs, one was behind a bullet-proof glass barrier at the entrance of a small administrative office to the right and a fourth - this one obviously an Italian soldier - stood in green fatigues and beret behind a four-foot pile of sandbags holding a small Beretta Model 12 machine gun, capable of pumping thirty-six bits of lead into a man in just under a second. Above the entrance was a sign printed in two languages. Jack read the English: *HEADQUARTERS, ALLIED FORCES SOUTHERN EUROPE*. Below it, in four languages, was a smaller red and white sign: *WELCOME TO AFSOUTH POST*.

Walking towards the two *Carabinieri*, Jack wondered if either spoke English. They did not. They seemed to argue back and forth, while traffic backed up into the street, about what Jack wanted and who he should see. Finally, one of them escorted him to the small administrative office and an American Air Force sergeant.

"I need to call the University of... ah, what was the name?"

"Maryland?" said the short, blond sergeant. "La Verne?"

"La Verne! That's it. There's someone there I'm supposed to meet." Jack explained, noticing the white name tag - SSGT HARRIS - pinned to the sergeant's light blue uniform.

"You can use that phone right there. Do you have the number?"

"Yeah," said Jack pulling a torn piece of paper from his shirt pocket.

Two-five-five-nine. Jack's finger followed the dial back to its starting point, making sure it did not stick along the way.

"University of La Verne, may I help you?" The voice was friendly and feminine.

"Hello, may I speak to Professor Freeman?"

"Sure, just one minute, please." The phone clicked. He had been put on hold. He hated that. That's what he often did at the Metropolitan office when he had a wiseass client call about the fine print in his life insurance policy.

"Hello." Jack recognized the voice as that of the man he had met the previous day.

"Mr. Freeman?"

"Yes?"

"Jack Jeffrey. We met yesterday at the beach, remember?"

"Sure. In fact, I was just thinking about you."

"Wondering if I was going to show up?"

"Right. Look, I've got the article here. Are you at the front gate?"

"Yes. In the little... I guess it's the Pass Office."

"Okay, I'll be right down."

"Thank you." There was a click at the other end and an instant dial tone.

Jack waited ten minutes, watching truck drivers, British rock groups and Italian girlfriends going through the pass process. Not only did each person desiring to enter base have to fill out two documents and show some proof of identification, but someone working at the NATO post had to also sign them in and stay with them as long as they remained aboard.

Finally, Mike Freeman's familiar face popped through the open door.

"Morning. Or is it afternoon?" he said, looking up at the large oval clock hanging above a tiny rectangular window.

"Hi," Jack replied.

"Okay, here's that article. You can keep it if you'd like."

"You're sure? Do you have other copies?"

"Sure, the day it came out I bought three papers."

"Okay. Well, I appreciate it."

"No problem at all. If I can do anything else for you, just call. You've got the number, and if I'm not there just leave a message." Mike extended his hand and Jack met it with his own.

"Thanks again."

(2)

The return train to Baia was practically empty. Jack had taken a seat on the outer edge of the aisle and now anxiously unfolded the newspaper. *THE INTERNATIONAL DAILY NEWS*, he read at the top of the front page. *AN INDEPENDENT DAILY NEWSPAPER SERVING ITALY, THE COMMON MARKET, MEDITERRANEAN, AND THE MIDDLE EAST.* He was not interested in past news and quickly turned the thin pages to the center section which had been dedicated to "THE ARTS". Mingled among two pages of opera reviews, movie listings, and a feature on Milan fashions, was the article that Jack sought: *THE TOMB OF APOLLO.* Just under the title, set in a smaller cursive type, was the subtitle: *Does this ancient mystery still exist?* Enthusiastically, Jack read on.

*Naples - for centuries, historians have sought to put together the puzzle that would lead them to the mythological treasures that were supposed to have been buried in the tomb of Apollo with the remains of the god's mortal love, Iosis. Recent studies have indicated that the ancient tomb did, in fact, exist in the region now known as the Phlegrean Fields, along the Mediterranean coast just west of Naples. Research has further pinpointed the location to that known as **Baia** and **Bacoli** today.*

*There are a number of theories that there was a direct relationship between the tomb and the ancient Sibyl that lived in the Acropolis at **Cumae**, though, to date, there is no real evidence of such a connection or what the tie might have been.*

Through early Greek scripts, the Archeology Department of the University of Naples has verified that the tomb existed during the Fourth Century B.C. and that it contained what the documents called the "gold of the gods."

According to Dr. Antonio Lombardi, director of antiquities in Naples, "The probability of the existence of such a tomb is excellent. This is a rich area for archeological finds and man will probably never discover everything that has been left behind by past civilizations. So, the chances of such a discovery are no more far-fetched than those of discovering the skeletons of fifteen people and a horse in Herculaneum, which were found earlier this year."

Because the tomb's existence is based on brief accounts in what scholars have categorized as unreliable mythological writings, many believe that an organized search at this point would be like hunting for the Golden Fleece. At the same time, however, many scholars feel that the ancient myths are perhaps one of the finest factual records of early Greek topography, history and societies.

As pointed out by Dr. Lombardi, "In 1870, archeologist Heinrich Schliemann discovered the city of Troy using the writings of Greek myths as a guide. If such a discovery as this is possible, why then do many experts continue to shun the probable existence of Apollo's tomb?"

(3)

"Hey! You guys turn into lobsters yet?" Jack said as he rushed across the beach, the hot sand seeping into his sandals, burning his feet.

"Not yet," replied Becky with a smile.

Valerie rolled over onto her back, squinting to keep out the blinding sun as she looked up at her husband. "Get the article?"

"Yeah." There was a short silence as Valerie adjusted the colorful beach towel beneath her.

"Well?"

"Well, what?" Jack asked.

"Well, was it worth the trip?"

"It sure was."

Jack plopped down in the green and red striped folding chair, under the shade of the umbrella. He gazed up at the villa. It looked like a tiny castle painted white. His brother had always had a keen taste for homes with personality. And, after his books became bestsellers, he also had the money it took to buy them.

On the train, he had torn the article out of the newspaper and folded it into his shirt breast pocket. Now, as he reached to retrieve it, he suddenly stopped. His eyes were still focused upwards towards the mountain. But it was not the villa that had caught his attention this time.

"Jack, did Jenny say when she would be home?" Valerie's eyes were still closed as she murmured the words and waited for a reply that did not come. "Jack?"

"Honey?" He had heard her the first time, but his intense concentration would not allow him to answer. He had gazed at the mountain a hundred times since they first began to come to the beach. This was the first time, however, that Jack noticed anyone on the mountain side. He had only caught a glimpse of what looked like an old woman, before she disappeared into a tall thicket of brush just a short distance from the house.

"Jack, are you listening to me?"

"Sure, honey... no, Jenny didn't say anything. Oh, wait a minute, yes, she did. She said she'd probably be late and not to wait for her for dinner."

Valerie did not move, but continued to lie, as if sleeping, in the sun. Becky, too, was lying on her stomach on a bright red towel. Jack, however, could not relax. There was something about the figure on the hill that he could not put his finger on. Something sinister. Something he did not like. Particularly so since it was so close to the villa. Jenny had warned him of thieves in the area. Maybe they were breaking in?

"Valerie. I'm going up to the house. You guys can stay here if you want. I want to catch up on some reading," he said, not wanting to alarm his wife and daughter. "I still haven't finished that western."

"Okay," said Valerie without looking up. "What time is it?"

"Twelve fifteen."

"We've got some sandwiches in the backpack. Want to eat something before you go?"

"No, I'm not hungry."

"Okay, we'll stay here a couple more hours then come up. You want to go, Becky?"

"No, the sun feels so good."

"Jack," Valerie called after him as he began to walk away. "Do you have the key?"

"Yeah. And you? I've got one in the bag. But you'll be there, won't you?"

"Sure."

"Then I won't need mine."

"Okay, see you later." Jack raced across the sand following the tracks he had left earlier. If someone was in the house he would have to hurry. It would take a good fifteen minutes to get up the hill.

(4)

Jack came up the west side steps and tried the door. It was locked. He was out of breath from his rapid climb. Slowly, he walked to the north side of the villa and around the east. Every door that led into the house was locked, and there was no evidence that anyone had attempted to enter. There was no possible way to enter from the south, since the balcony hung over the edge of the mountain.

Jack stopped at the top of the cliff and looked down at the beach where his family lay motionless, like miniature toys.

Strange, he thought. He had seen someone. Whoever it had been was not at the villa. His mind had probably been overly imaginative to conjure up the thought of the place being burglarized. Still, the figure had been just below the villa down the side of this cliff. What would anyone be doing down there? He paused for a couple of minutes, then walked to the right where the earth had eroded, leaving a trench that could be easily used to climb down the side of the mountain. There was only one way to find out what the figure was doing below the villa and that was to go there himself.

The initial descent seemed easy until Jack's foot slipped, causing him to skid down ten feet of hard, dry dirt, finally stopping in a thicket of briars. Painfully, he stood up, brushed off his clothes and began to ease towards the right to where he had seen the figure earlier. The pocket of his shirt sleeve was torn and two buttons had been popped off as a result of the fall. His stomach also carried a flesh-less patch of blood seeping scrapes. It was not enough to stop him however.

As his eyes came across the dark hole cut out of the ground, though, he did stop. It was the size of a small refrig-erator door. Because of the angle, the cave entrance could not be seen from the beach. But Jack was sure that it was through here that the figure had disappeared.

He looked up. The villa was directly overhead, its balcony hanging over him. Maybe it had been kids playing in the cave? Jack looked into the pit. There were steps leading downwards and something glistened at the bottom. Though he had always feared entering dark, unknown places, his curiosity to explore this place was overtaking him.

Slowly, he picked his way along. Perhaps there were snakes living in there. He stopped. Perspiration was dripping from his forehead and his stomach was beginning to hurt.

The sun, which had been hidden beneath a fluffy white altostratus cloud, now came out in full force. Jack could suddenly see a room below him as light beamed through the opening. With a new confidence he leaped to the mosaic floor. His physical ailments were forgotten as he stood eyeing the room. It was a tomb. His early archeological studies had given him enough insight to recognize the design and minute tesserae that made up the patterns of the interior. Yes. There was no doubt. He had discovered a tomb of some sort.

It took five minutes before Jack's eyes adjusted to the semi-darkness. By that time he had also noticed the almost gagging odor. And, as his enthusiasm lessened, he saw that the tomb continued at one end, heading to another underground section. He shuffled over to investigate the opening. It was not large enough to go through erect. But, on his hands and knees, he could manage to crawl past the hunks of loose earth. Like an infant, he eased forward, feeling his way along the opening and into the adjacent room. This place was not like the other. It was small. Its walls and floors were hard, packed dirt. Jack could tell this much from the feel of the smooth surface.

Then, his body became rigid. It was as if he had frozen, except for the continuous trembling that now controlled his nerves. In front of him was an open doorway. On the opposite side of the door was a light. A light that someone had forgotten to turn off. And, in the light, he recognized the basement of Jennifer's villa. He had entered the basement through an unknown passage. At least unknown to himself. The story of Valerie seeing someone in the basement flashed like a photograph past his mind's eye. Had she really seen someone here?

The door rested at an angle, hanging by its top hinge. It had not been like this when Jack found Valerie here. But who had ripped it from its supports?

The question was beginning to churn through his head when a smell of rotting flesh pierced his nostrils. It was the smell that had been in the house, but now stronger, and its source was neither known nor could it be seen. But it had to be there. He covered his mouth and nose with the tail of his shirt. It was slightly wet from the sweat, but he didn't mind. His own odor was sweet compared to that which filtered through the air. He searched the entire basement with his eyes, but the darkness at the opposite end kept him from seeing everything. The scorching scent was infiltrating his lungs with every breath of hot muggy air. There was definitely something there.

As he entered, the door made a scream on its single hinge, sounding like a woman being raped in a New York alley. Almost total darkness engulfed the far end of the basement with the exception of a slit of protruding light, like a heavenly ray, from the tiny bulb.

His eyes watered. A burning sensation clung to his nostrils. Convulsively his chest heaved up and down like a fish out of water. A chilling stream of perspiration trickled down his armpits, down his sides, finally resting on the waistline of his Levis. The salt in his sweat burned the scrape along his stomach.

The smell was everywhere, a constant rot. It seemed as if the cellar itself were dead. Cobwebs stuck like stretched taffy to his mouth, nose, and eyes as he stalked through the room towards the darkness.

There was a corner where the smell seemed to grow stronger. Jack stopped. The ceiling was lower there. He would have to crouch to examine it.

He had taken five steps, and not long ones, when he felt and heard the soft crunching beneath his foot.

By now the gagging odor seemed to be poisoning him. Tears rolled from his eyes and from his nose ran a constant flow of mucus. Jack reached into his pocket and brought out the pack of matches he had used that morning to light the gas stove. Fumbling in the dark, he struck one. In the flickering light he could see that the object under his foot was the cause of his physical distress. The body of a large mutilated gray cat lay there, rotting. Patches of hair were scattered in every direction, like the stuffing of a child's toy pet. Maggots surfaced hurriedly through the old cat's nose and mouth, eating away at the carcass. Flies licked the intestines, which were covered in saliva, and crawled about the blood-soaked organs as if they were attending a dinner of chicken and mashed potatoes. Mucus dripped from one eye while the other glared, bulging into the light.

As he gazed upon the hideous sight a pain like lightning shot through his head. Vomit heaved from his wincing stomach onto his sandal covered foot. He had found the smell. But, he had also discovered something that left a mystery in his reeling head - a mystery only Jennifer could solve.

VALERIE

(1)

It was always hot in the old villa, but this evening when Valerie and Becky returned from the beach it was unbearable. The odor that had been lingering for the past few days was now enough to turn their stomachs.

"Becky, open some windows!"

"In the kitchen?"

"Everywhere! And leave the door open. Jack!" She waited. There was no reply. The door had been locked. Where was he? "Jack! Where are you?"

"Becky, open the big windows in the library. But make sure the latch is set so they don't bang shut."

"Okay," her daughter replied, heading down the hallway.

"Where the hell is he?" Valerie whispered to herself.

Fifteen minutes passed before Jack came through the front door, dirty and smelling like a garbage dump. Valerie had already hung the beach towels and bathing suits in the bathroom and was preparing dinner when he appeared.

"Where have you been?"

"You wouldn't believe me if I told you. I can't believe it myself."

She looked at her husband. He was pale and perspiration rolled from his brow. She didn't know what had happened, but he had definitely been through something.

"Jack, what happened?" After what she had been through the previous week he had his doubts about whether he should tell her.

"Later. Right now all I want to do is take a shower and get this stink off me."

Jack passed his daughter, who was coming out of her bedroom, as he went up the stairs. With his mind totally absorbed by his discoveries, he did not even notice her. Becky watched him disappear in the upstairs hall and proceeded into the kitchen.

"What's wrong with Dad?"

"I don't know."

"He smells like he fell in the sewer."

"Shut up and fix the table." Valerie was worried about her husband. Where had he been? And why did he look so sick?

(2)

By the time dinner was over, the three of them were ready for bed. It had been a hot day and the sun had sapped most of their energy. It was only eight thirty and Jennifer had not yet returned, but they were just too tired to wait any longer. All, that is, except Jack.

He had still not told his wife of the discovery. And, by the time they were in bed, Valerie's curiosity had grown to the point of exploding.

"Jack, are you going to tell me what happened today?" Her look was stern, determined and he realized he could not keep it a secret any longer. Slowly he explained his adventure in every detail. Valerie listened with awe as he told of the tomb, which led to the cellar and the dead cat. Finally, when he had finished, she moved close to him and cuddled against his chest.

"What do you think?"

"I don't know."

The memory of her own incident in the cellar and the creature popped vividly into her mind along with the terrifying realization that it might not have been her imagination at all.

"Jack, I forgot to close the big windows in the library."

"Don't worry about it. Jenny'll do it when she comes in. Let's try to get some sleep. Tomorrow I want to go down there again. I also want to talk to Jenny. She knew about this. I just wonder how much more she knows and isn't telling us.

JENNIFER IV

It was late when Jennifer returned. By now the steady breeze coming from the open window had carried the smell out of the villa. Her breath had a distinct smell of liquor. And, for the first time in six years, she was drunk.

It had taken her longer than expected to find what she wanted. But, after hours of walking through the Via Mancini district - better known as "Thieves' Alley" - she finally met someone who could help her. She had paid well for the merchandise. But in the price was also the fact that there were no traces of her identity left behind as there would have been had she purchased it through normal channels.

Staggering, she went directly to her bedroom, closed the door, and began searching for the large, leather handbag.

"Where're you...lil' bastard. I'll show 'em." Her words were slurred as if she was half asleep.

Finally, her fingers touched the small package, gripped it and pulled it from its hiding place. The bag plopped onto the floor as Jennifer fell heavily onto the bed, the package still in her clutches. She let out a long intoxicated sigh and began systematically unwrapping the package: first the thin twine, then the outer brown paper, and finally, the white tissue. A smaller box fell onto the light blue sheet that covered the bed. In her hand she now held the shiny black Beretta model 70 pistol. It was small, sleek and perfect for a woman. In her fogged mind, she could picture herself using it.

"Powwww. Powwww... hah, hah, hah..!" She fired off imaginary blasts at her reflection in the mirror. But this was not the target she was after.

Excited, she got up, snatched the smaller box from the floor and once again took her place on the sagging mattress. She ripped the thin white paper off, revealing a small green and red box containing twenty 7.65mm cartridges.

Three nights before, she had returned to the cellar while the others were asleep. What she found terrified her even more than the initial discovery that the creature escaped. The heavy door, which she had struggled so hard to close, had once again been pried open, this time the lock had been broken completely. The creature had returned. It could now enter the cellar at will.

The thought sent chills through Jennifer, causing her shoulders to hunch and her whole body to shudder. There were still two doors that stopped the beast from getting into the main house.

"Maybe tomorrow," she giggled to herself in a drunken whisper. "Maybe only one more night and we'll not have to worry about it *anymore*." She toyed with the pistol, turning it over and over in her hands. "Everyone will be out...except me...*huh-huh, huh-huh*," she chuckled to herself. "And when it comes in to hide...*yes...yes...hah- hah*...I'll find it. If not tomorrow, the next day. But I'll find it...*huh, huh-huh...*"

THE CREATURE II

(1)

For two days the creature had found refuge in a cubby hole, returning to the cellar periodically to check the dead cat. Its new lair, just north of the villa, was not as large as the old, but it was a perfect observation point. And it was here that the beast lay, its belly flat against the cool earth, watching, when Jennifer staggered up the long steps.

The squeaking sound of the rusted gate hinges caused the creature's ears to perk up. Its beady eyes pierced the darkness, catching Jennifer's unstable movements. A gurgle came from its throat sounding like a gagging infant. Slowly, the swollen lips parted and cracked as the beast smiled. Saliva seeped through the rotting teeth and dripped from one corner of the gaped mouth. It continued to watch Jennifer, study her, examine her every move. Then, once the woman was safely in the house, it began crawling out of the hole. Its legs worked like those of a swimming frog, kicking and kicking until it had escaped the confines of the new den.

Silently, the hunched beast crept around the villa, observing every door, window and possible opening that could act as an entrance. On the western side, it found what it was after. There were two long glass doors, like those used for patios. One of them had been left open. Not much, perhaps less than eight inches. But, it was enough for the bone-like creature to slither through and into the luxurious home.

As it walked it made a shuffling sound and its nails clicked on the marble pavement. Along its path, an air of putrid odor remained in its wake. Tonight, it would not venture through the villa as it had in the past. It knew that Becky was in the bedroom beside the kitchen and that Jack and Valerie were in the upstairs room. But, it was not them the creature sought. It was the woman of the ancient home. The owner. The hideous hag that stalked these echoing halls of death... the murderer. Jennifer! It would be a battle of the beasts! Jennifer! Jennifer the assassin! Jennifer the murderer! Jennifer the beast! Jennifer against the creature of the dark! The creature of the cellar! Creature of the tomb!

The hideous beast trembled with anticipated excitement as it neared the woman's room. Its nose rose until it was sticking up towards the ceiling. A distinct fragrance came from around the closed door. The fragrance of Jennifer! The smile returned to the pale, deathlike face. Its eyes glistening with excitement.

It reached out with its lizard-like hand, the infected scabs - from its battle with the cat - oozing pus as the skin tightened. It was unlocked. Swiftly, the creature entered, leaving the door open behind it.

Through the darkness, it recognized the sleeping woman. A smell of alcohol lingered in the air. It hated the smell. It was the smell of death. But, it would be gone soon.

Silently, the beast moved to Jennifer's bedside. For a long time it gazed upon the woman, still clothed and panting in a drunken sleep.

A long, thin, clear trickle of saliva slid from the creature's parted lips and onto Jennifer's bare arm. She did not stir. As the burning odor of human excrement began to flow through her nostrils, however, her eyes opened.

In an instant, Jennifer relived a visual account of the murder she had committed six years earlier, in all its hot, red blood and steaming guts. Her eyes bulged from their sockets causing the blood vessels around the edges to burst, shooting splotches of red through the creamy white. Her face grew pure white, like freshly fallen snow. The skin that covered her skull drew taut and the fine hairs that grew on the back of her neck prickled.

Jennifer opened her eyes to see, above her horrified face, at a distance of not more than ten inches, the face of the beast. It hovered over her, its split tongue hanging out, drooling smelly spit over the woman. Deep giggles belched from its gullet. Gobs of matted hair dangled over her like the snakes of Medusa. The beast's breath odor of rotting flesh bellowed from its nose and mouth over Jennifer as if she had stuck her head into a clogged toilet that had been used for weeks.

Screams of terror ripped through the black chambers of Jennifer's mind. Her skull was bursting from the exploding sound. She was killing herself with fear. It was eating her, like a rat trying to chew out her brain. The terror was not due to any aspect of the creature's grotesque physical appearance. It was with telepathic ability that the beast's eyes beamed into the woman's head. Words could not be formed in the creature's mouth. But through its eyes Jennifer could hear it speaking.

"Vengeance. The time has come. Vengeance. Death. Death to the murderer! Vengeance! Vengeance! Vengeance! *VENGEANCE! DEATH! DEATH! DEATH!!!*"

Jennifer watched as the creature's thin, brown, leathery arm rose. Its eyes were now watery, glistening and turned up into its head so all that remained was white. Its lips were turned back, the four rotting teeth showing against the wide open mouth like the fangs of a vampire. Saliva now covered the creature's neck, dripping down over a pair of shriveled, milkless breasts.

A ray of moonlight beamed through the window giving Jennifer a perfect view of the four razor sharp, knife-like fingernails as they came ripping through the air towards her thin, white, stretched throat.

"*AHHHHHHHHH*!" The cry was cut short as the piercing fingernails sunk two inches into the vulnerable flesh. She felt a blow, hard and forceful. Then a warm needle pricking through her head. Then relief. The force was no longer there. Her mouth was open, but she did not need it to breathe. Air eased out of her lungs and surfaced through the new openings in her trachea. She could no longer feel her legs, then hips, chest, and arms.

THUD! The beast struck again! This time the nails closed on the ravaged breathing tube and pulled, tugging and tugging at the human vine.

Jennifer's last gasp of life had now reached the brain. And with it, words formed in her mind: "*I...I'm...dead*!"

(2)

It had taken Jack and Valerie five minutes to get downstairs from the time they were awakened by the blood curdling wail that Jennifer had let out. Now, in the dimly lit hallway, Jack stood staring in at the lifeless figure on the bed. His wife stood a few feet behind him, clinging to Becky. Jack reached, slowly, inside the arched doorway and flipped the light switch.

"Go to the kitchen!" he yelled at his wife and daughter. There was no need for them to see what he hypnotically gazed upon. It was Jennifer. Her head was nearly severed from the rest of her body. Blood was everywhere, swiped across the sheet, soaking the mattress, spread around the floor, and smeared on the night stand. In some places Jack noticed it was a bright, almost scarlet, red, while in other spots it was dark, a kind of purple color.

"What is it, Jack?" Valerie's voice did not break his trance. He stood rigid, trembling. His heart was pounding as if seeking a way to escape its confinement. He did not even hear his wife coming into the room.

"*AHHHHHhhhh...!*" She had seen Jennifer.

Instantly Jack whirled, pushing her back into the hallway. "I told you to go into the kitchen! Now get in there!"

The scream had brought him back to his senses. It also caused the creature to stir in the far corner of Jennifer's bedroom.

A warm sensation ran through Jack as his ears picked up the sound. His entire body shook with fear. Whatever or whoever had done this to Jennifer was still there. He whirled and his eyes got their first look at the creature. At the same time the beast's smell struck him. He waited, but the human-looking beast did not advance. A blubbering sound came from its mouth as if it were trying to communicate. Though the face was horrid to look upon, Jack continued to stare. If it moved, he was ready as he snatched a long-necked glass vase from the dresser top. But the beast did not move. The bony fingers, dripping with fresh blood, covered its ugly face. One minute passed in silence. Then, Jack heard soft cries coming from the crouched, naked figure. It was crying.

"What do you want?" he whispered.

The creature looked up, its eyes red and swollen. Tears flowed down the thin face. Its arms extended towards him as if asking for comfort. It turned its head so that light illuminated it perfectly.

For a moment, Jack thought he was going insane. Memories kept flashing in his head as he looked at the pleading creature. Memories of pictures. A *flash*. The creature. Another *flash*. Again the creature. A *flash*! The creature! *Flash*! Creature! *FLASH*! CREATURE! *FLASH*! It turned over and over and over in his head! THE PICTURE!!! The circuits finally connected in his human computer, giving him the answer that his subconscious had sought.

The beast was horrible, smelled of decay, and was a putrefied example of a human being. But there was something else, the something that had caused him to pick his brain. On the left hand side of the creature's face was a slash of red. Not blood, but a discoloration of the skin. A birthmark. The exact birthmark that Jack had seen in the picture of his dead niece.

He took two steps towards the sobbing creature. It looked directly at him. Its mouth was now closed. A sad look had taken over its features. Its arms now wrapped around itself as if to hide its nakedness.

There was no doubt in his mind. Jack was looking into the eyes of Angelica.

ANGELICA II

t was 5:45 a.m. and three blue and white Alfa-Romeos were parked outside the white stucco villa at 14/*A Via Roma*. On the side of the vehicles was the word *Polizia*. The second red and white ambulance from the Nuovo Policlinico had just pulled away with the creature that had once been the young, petite Angelica. The first ambulance had left five minutes earlier carrying the remains of the girl's mother. Also in the dirt road was the large black sedan that Tom Robinson, the U.S. Vice Consulate of Naples and Mario Vita, his interpreter, had come in.

Neighbors had begun to gather around the outer fence, trying to discover what had happened. Valerie and Becky were upstairs packing. Police had combed the villa top to bottom and were still going over Jennifer's room for evidence. Jack stood on the front steps with three other men discussing the events that had taken place through the night and the past six years.

"You mean she's lived in that tiny cellar room for all this time?" asked Jack.

"Evidently so," said Tom Robinson. "What they think is that Mrs. Jeffrey killed her husband and kept the girl...what's her name?"

"Angelica."

"Angelica, in the cellar. I know it sounds insane, but it's not the first time such a thing has been discovered after a number of years."

"*E la lingua!*" expressed Doctor Mario Milano, who had examined Angelica before they had taken her away.

"What's that?" Jack asked.

"He said, the tongue," explained the interpreter.

"Evidently," interrupted Robinson, "the girl's tongue had been split at the end some time ago. Perhaps the same night your brother was killed."

"What will happen to her now?"

The interpreter spoke for a few moments with the doctor then turned to Jack. "He says that physically they can get her back to a stable condition in a few months."

"And mentally?"

"Her mind has been badly disturbed. Doctor Milano is not a psychiatrist, but he feels that the girl will never be able to comprehend people or things that take place around her again. At least not in the sense of understanding that we know it."

"We'll get you in the Vesuvius Hotel," said Robinson. "It's not far from our office. The documents will be ready to sign this afternoon at two. We'll try to get the facts straight and everything sorted out as soon as possible so that you and your family can return to Michigan."

"Thank you," Jack sighed, looking up into the distance. The silhouette of Pozzuoli looked like a postcard as the sun began to come up over the eastern horizon. It was going to be a beautiful day. He could not forget the creature...Angelica in the corner of the bedroom. Reaching out to him for help. Pleading. Begging.

EPILOGUE

On November 27th, Angelica Jeffrey was transferred from the Naples Nuovo Policlinico and admitted into the Ospedale Civile di S. Leonardo in the province of Castellamare di Stabia, where she would remain for the rest of her life under the constant care of a trained psychiatrist.

It was 8:15 a.m. when the tall, dark-haired nurse wheeled Angelica from the ambulance into the new hospital.

Maria Esposito was just getting off duty. It had been a quiet night, allowing her time to read the ancient history book she had picked up at the Biblioteca Comunale on Corso Garibaldi the previous day. She had changed into her civilian clothes and was about to leave the hospital when she noticed Angelica being pushed towards her.

Maria stopped suddenly. The book, which had been braced between her side and upper arm, fell to the floor. As Angelica came closer, the girl began to tremble. Her nerves raced, sending warm sensations from her feet through her head as if a thousand stinging syringe needles were stabbing her systematically. When the wheelchair was within three steps from her, Angelica looked up, meeting the nurse's eyes with her own. She could feel herself growing faint as the invalid girl's stare shot like piercing arrows into her soul. It was as if Maria knew the secret. The secret of this creature. The secret that now the two of them shared.

The nurse stood for some time after the wheelchair passed and Angelica had disappeared into a room at the end of the hall. Maria still felt weak. Until now, she had been unable to move, frozen to the sleek, polished floor. Slowly, she staggered to the wooden bench along the wall. She bent, retrieved the heavy, brown covered book of ancient Greek history and placed it into her lap. It was ten minutes before she had built up enough courage to open the book to the place she had marked the night before. Finally, her hands trembling, she flipped to page 273. There, she saw something that caused her lower lip to quiver and eyes to grow into enormous, bulging egg shapes.

At the top of the page, in thick Old English letters, was written: *THE SIBYL OF CUMAE.* Below this was a black and white drawing of a thin-faced, dark-eyed woman identical to that of the patient that had glared at her from the wheelchair.

An eerie shudder passed down Maria Esposito's back as she read the caption under the staring drawing.

SHE WAS MUTE, BUT COULD SPEAK TO ALL WITH HER MIND. AND ONCE THE TOMB HAD BEEN DEFENDED, THE PHYSICAL BEING, WHICH THEY KNEW AS THE SIBYL OF CUMAE, FELL FROM HER PERCH. SHE HAD FINALLY DIED. BUT HER SPIRIT WOULD LIVE FOREVER. FOREVER, IN THE CHAIN OF ENDLESS SIBYLS.

A note from the author: Thank you for allowing me to take up some of your time with *The Oracle*. I sincerely hope you have enjoyed this work of fiction and that you will consider reading my future works like *Deathwatch*, which is scheduled for release very soon.

Please feel free to send me an email with your comments, good and bad, on this book or anything else that might fancy you. I can be reached at msedge@thesedgegroup.com.

Sincerely,

Michael Sedge